The Apartment

by

Khushboo Yadav

The Apartment
by Khushboo Yadav

ISBN: 978-93-62206-60-2

Published by

DOUBLE 9 BOOKS

2/13-B, Ansari Road
Daryaganj, New Delhi – 110002
info@double9books.com
www.double9books.com
Tel. 011-40042856

ABOUT THE AUTHOR

Khushboo Yadav, a budding writer born in Mumbai, India, dedicates her spare time to crafting short stories and novels. Prior to delving into novel writing, she worked as a freelance writer, gaining valuable experience in the field. Currently, she serves as a Quality Analyst at an IT firm. Despite her professional commitments, Khushboo remains passionate about her writing pursuits, using her creativity to weave captivating tales that resonate with readers. Inspired by her upbringing in the vibrant city of Mumbai, she infuses her stories with rich cultural elements and authentic experiences. Khushboo journey as a writer reflects her dedication and determination to pursue her literary ambitions alongside her professional responsibilities. With each story she creates, she continues to refine her craft and connect with audiences through her imaginative storytelling.

CONTENTS

This is for you, Siddhant.

CHAPTER 1
COINCIDENCE OR CHANCE?

Samrat perceived this day as indistinguishable from any other in his dull routine at the department. As a police officer, he found himself involved with a handful of pending cases, which he felt lacked excitement or intrigue. Whether dealing with robbery, domestic violence (which often resolved itself), or minor incidents, he remained dispassionate about the tasks at hand. Frequently, he wanted to reflect on his desire for frivolous and unfounded cases to prove his capability. After reviewing the files, he'd nonchalantly toss them on his desk, convinced that they were a mere waste of his time. His discontentment with the department's lack of initiative led him to grumble about it while scanning through local news.

The cycle continued, and he'd flip back and forth between the newspaper and a small diary, which he would idly doodle in. As he waited for something eventful to happen, he also fiddled with a triangular glass showpiece to pass the time. Restless and bored after sitting in the same spot for an hour, he yearned for more stimulating challenges. While crime was a common occurrence, nothing seemed significant enough to pique his interest.

"What a lazy day!" he exclaimed, his hand scribbling hastily in his small diary.

"Aye!" chimed in another officer after Samrat's outburst.

"And the weather's gloomy too. I should have taken the day off today, you know. Stayed home, watched TV, and had some pizza," Samrat grumbled in annoyance.

"You're absolutely right, Officer Chauhan. I can relate," Officer Rao agreed.

"But you don't often go home, do you?" Officer Rao continued, jokingly.

"Why do you care?" Samrat asked, eyeing him suspiciously.

"It's none of your business, I suppose." he continued.

In a fit of frustration, Samrat tore a page from his diary and tossed it at Officer Rao.

"Stop coating your sentences with sarcasm, Officer Rao," he retorted.

"Oh, I'm just agreeing with you," Officer Rao replied casually.

"Thank you for your support, but..." Samrat began, but his phone rang, interrupting him.

"Hello, Officer Chauhan here..." Samrat answered the phone but his expression suddenly changed. He grabbed the diary he had been doodling in a few minutes ago, along with a pen, and hastily jotted down an address.

"Don't worry, ma'am. I'll be there in a minute," he assured the caller before hanging up. Though he tried to hide it, there was a sense of satisfaction within him, knowing that the rest of the day would be spent on an investigation. He glanced at Officer Rao, his face void of emotion but brimming with anticipation.

Grabbing his old goggles, Samrat left his desk and headed toward the door before going out from the police station. As he made his way out, Officer Rao called out to him.

"Looks like you've got a fish on the hook," he remarked.

Samrat turned a blind eye to him continuing on his way, but this time he couldn't suppress a small smile, however, he tried to escape it from his lips, with the feeling that something exciting was coming his way, something about to embark on an intriguing adventure. He looked at Officer Rao, no expression on his face but anticipation inside of his mind. Retrieving his old goggles, he departs from his desk. Before exiting the police station, Officer Rao calls out to Samrat.

"Shut up," he retorts in irritation.

Officer Rao chuckles at Samrat's reaction.

"Aren't you forgetting something?" he teases, glancing at Samrat's desk.

"What?" Samrat questions.

"Your diary... or your notebook," Officer Rao points towards the diary.

Officer Rao rises from his chair and moves towards Samrat's table. Anticipating Officer Rao's intentions, Samrat hastily reaches for his desk and tightly clutches his diary.

"Easy, man!" Officer Rao says, trying to ease the tension.

"I don't trust you, not even a bit," Samrat comments, holding onto his diary protectively.

Finding everything in order, he decided to check out the lady who had called him.

Samrat entered the building and searched for apartment number 201. He knocked on the door, but there was no response. He knocked again. Still no answer.

"Should I break in?" Samrat thought, that breaking in would be a bad idea as he recalled one of the incidents where he and Officer Rao were investigating a case.

Wondering whether he should break in, he recalled the department's training, which advised against such actions during investigations to avoid jeopardizing their status and career.

During their training, they were instructed not to forcefully enter any civilian's premises during investigations. Violating this rule could potentially harm their reputation and career. Officer Chauhan initially considered this directive to be a foolish attempt by the department to express condolences to the victim's family. However, given his position and past experiences, he eventually arrived at a different conclusion. He thought to wait for a few seconds and press the doorbell button one more time yet there was no response so he recalled the phone that he received at the police station and contemplated contacting the station to retrieve the number. But before he could leave the scene, the door suddenly unlocked, and a lady cautiously opened it, revealing only her eyes peering out.

"Who are you?" the old lady's voice sounded frail.

"I'm Officer Samrat Chauhan. I received a call from this address," he introduced himself. "What was the emergency?"

"Did I call you?" she questioned.

"Yes."

"When?" she asked.

"About an hour ago, I believe. Is everything okay, ma'am?" Samrat asked.

"I don't recall making any call. Is everything alright, Officer?" she continued.

"I'm assuming it's fine, but I still need to look around your apartment, ma'am," he said.

"You may come inside," she granted him entry.

Despite being in her 60s, the lady had an aura of elegance. Her almond eyes sparkled, and she had long, thin, untied gray hair that gave her a certain radiance. With a round face and a graceful glow, she looked remarkably beautiful for her age. She brushed her hair forward, partially hiding a mark on her neck.

"You can check around, but please do it quickly. I'm a very busy lady. Do you understand, Officer?" she spoke firmly.

"Of course, ma'am," he replied.

Samrat stepped into the apartment and immediately noticed a painting resting against the wall, rather than being hung. It depicted a star inside a circle. As he approached the painting, the old lady warned him not to get too close. An unusual feeling overcame him when he took a few steps nearer to the painting. There was also a table in front of the couch, with some scrambled papers, a small stack of murder-related novels, and a small diary on the floor that looked identical to Samrat's own diary. He turned to the lady with a puzzled expression, hoping to receive an appropriate explanation.

"Please don't touch that painting. I have to return it," she requested.

"The painting?" he inquired.

"Yes, and those are..." she pointed to the table.

"That is work-related. Don't worry," she assured him.

"What's your name?" he asked.

"Ahilya Mathur," she replied.

Taking out his diary, he jotted down her name. Continuing his search, he picked up the scrambled papers, hoping to find a clue, but he refrained from reading them and simply kept some in his pocket. Despite looking around the room, he found nothing else of significance except for those papers. He then turned his attention to the diary. However, just as he was about to open it, a shattering sound echoed from the kitchen. He quickly rushed to investigate and found broken pieces of glass on the floor.

"Are you alright?" he asked with concern.

The lady nodded and continued picking up the broken glass. Samrat thought of offering his assistance, but she politely declined. While surveying the kitchen, he noticed some sticky notes on the refrigerator. He approached to examine the details written on them and took note of phrases like 'Call the police.'

"Call the police?" he questioned with curiosity. "What does this mean?"

"Oh, they are just my thoughts and ideas for a novel. You know, I'm writing a crime drama," she explained.

"A novel?" Samrat expressed his disinterest.

"Yes, though I haven't decided on the title yet," she said.

"Well, novels aren't my cup of tea," he remarked.

As he checked out some more notes on the refrigerator, he noticed phrases like 'writing a novel', 'crime drama novel.', 'call the police', and 'mention date every day'

"Oh! You should try reading some; they can kill time," she suggested.

He turned back to face her.

"By the way, do you live alone here?"

"Yes," she confirmed.

Samrat made a note of this in his diary.

"Do you own this house?" he inquired.

"Yes," she replied.

Samrat made a note of this detail once again.

"Not precisely. My son used to live here. He owns the house with me. But then he got shifted to some other place," she explained.

"He owns the house with you?" Samrat sought clarification.

"Yes, we are co-owners," she replied.

"Do you know where your son resides now?" Samrat inquired further.

"Oh, I don't remember. I have a weak memory," she admitted.

"I can see that," Samrat remarked.

Feeling confused about the whole situation, Samrat considered asking her about the call he received from her earlier.

"I received a call from your end. It was related to a crime that you mentioned in a trembling tone. I'm afraid you are aware of that," Samrat explained.

"I don't remember making any call," she confirmed as she dumped the broken glasses into the bin.

"Somebody must have made a false call," she speculated.

"Probably. In that case, I believe everything is normal here," Samrat concluded.

"I'm sure of that," she said.

"Please allow me to leave," Samrat requested.

"Thank you, Officer..."

"No worries, you can call me Samrat," he replied politely.

She thanked him, and both of them left the kitchen. Samrat assumed it was a false call and decided to leave the apartment. However, his uncertainty still lingered, prompting him to turn back and ask her once again. But to his surprise, she had disappeared. It was strange since she had been standing right behind him just moments ago, watching him leave, but now she was nowhere to be found. Samrat wanted to clarify further, but his attempt to find her turned out to be a disappointment.

As he descended the stairs slowly, he couldn't shake off his curiosity about why she would make a false call. Determined to get answers, he planned to inquire again. However, before he could do so, he heard the lady shouting. He quickly rushed to her room following her voice. She was standing in front of her bedroom window, shouting frantically. Her wide eyes refused to blink, and her face had turned pale. She kept screaming, "Call the police!" over and over again.

"I am the police. Please calm down, ma'am," Samrat tried to soothe her.

"You see... there's all blood on the floor," she cried.

"What are you..." Samrat began to ask but was interrupted by her pointing her finger at a glass window, which led to an apartment opposite hers. Curious, Samrat went closer to the window, leaning forward to see the incident described by the lady. However, he found nothing but an empty apartment. There was no sign of any crime or disturbance. Perplexed by the situation, he tried looking through the window itself, but it didn't provide any answers. He couldn't fathom what was wrong with the lady.

After scratching his head in confusion for a moment, he reassured the lady twice that he would go and check the alleged crime scene according to her description.

Exasperated and cursing his day, he emerged from the apartment. However, he also felt the need to verify whether the lady's statements were true or if she was simply making his day worse. Without hesitation, he sprinted toward the apartment that was across from the lady's place, the very apartment where the alleged murder had taken place according to Ahilya's claim. Descending the stairs as fast as possible, he rushed straight to the location, only to find the place ravaged. Panting and infuriated, he realized there were no other residents around to question either. The location bore signs of fire damage, and the building itself seemed to be in a state of disrepair.

The apartment was the sole one on that floor, so he didn't bother to inquire with neighbors from other buildings about its occupants or owner. To him, it seemed that Ahilya was just wasting his time, and he wanted to escape from this situation that he had misunderstood as an opportunity.

"Could this day even get any worse?" he muttered in frustration.

Having captured no useful information, he considered his efforts a waste and headed back to his car. However, before reaching his vehicle, he decided to assure Ahilya that her perceptions were unfounded. He had thought of doing so earlier but had wanted to avoid any further contact with her, fearing she might make him even angrier. However, given his duty as an officer, he felt obliged to carry out his work and approached her apartment once more. This time, her door was half-open. Instead of entering, he called out for her.

"Hello, Mrs. Mathur."

Without any delay, she appeared at the door. "Yes?"

"There is no..." he began.

"Is everything okay, officer?" she asked, as though she had never seen him before.

Samrat was bewildered by her behavior, finding his perceptions and assumptions about Ahilya to be true. She seemed rather eccentric to him. Taking a deep breath, he calmed his senses and replied amiably, "Sorry for bothering you, ma'am. I was just patrolling in the area."

"Oh, no problem, officer. But you should be aware that people are not safe around here. You need to be vigilant," she said, sounding genuinely concerned. "I saw a man struggling for his life a few days ago."

"Where? Did you report it?" he inquired.

"Well, I don't remember exactly what happened after that. I only take notes," she explained.

"Notes. Did you see someone else...? I mean, along with that man?" Samrat asked.

"I don't recall clearly, but it happened in the apartment opposite from my apartment. It was visible from my bedroom window."

CHAPTER 2
THE RELATIONSHIP

On a consecutive weekend, Samrat spent dinner night with his wife Kanak, which was a rare occurrence. He typically preferred to devote most of his time to work, even during the night. Initially, Kanak was upset by her husband's neglectful behavior, but over time, she learned to accept it to some extent. Nevertheless, she tried various tactics to make Samrat stay at home, attempting online sessions, reading articles, and even attending small kitty parties to learn from other women how to control their husband's behavior and attitude. She even sought marriage counseling without Samrat's involvement.

During one of the kitty parties, she encountered women who claimed to have control over their husbands, although Kanak found the idea nonsensical. Her desire was not to dominate Samrat but rather to have him by her side, showing affection and caring for their relationship. The main purpose of attending such parties was to gather ideas, but she selectively filtered the suggestions, never staying at these gatherings for more than thirty minutes due to boredom. She never preferred to be around people.

One advice she received from an online session was to act depressed as a means to gain Samrat's attention, at least partially. While depression is a serious subject that captures everyone's attention and sympathy, using it to manipulate someone is an unethical act, though it bears no legal penalty. Kanak pretended to be distressed, and it did yield some results initially, but eventually, Samrat saw through her act, labeling it as mere drama.

"Babe, this is definitely not the way," he said calmly.

"Then how am I supposed to stop you?" she argued.

"You're not around, and it gets so lonely," she continued, expressing her frustration.

"I have a lot of cases to solve... you need to understand, it's my jo..." he tried to reason.

"IT'S MY JOB!" She shouted, interrupting him.

"It's always your job. Catching robbers? Solving domestic violence? What else is involved?" she continued, their familiar arguments repeating once or twice every week. Most of the time, they occurred over the phone, but occasionally in person when Samrat was at home. Kanak once attended a group counseling session where people of varying ages and backgrounds gathered to share their feelings. During the session, she talked about feeling isolated in her relationship but never mentioned her husband's name or his profession. Her attempts to fake depression, act distressed, and attend kitty parties for ideas had all proven futile, so she turned to the group for support. She believed sharing her emotions might help her maintain her mental and emotional well-being.

Initially, she found herself enjoying the sessions, not because she was genuinely interested but because she received new recommendations once again. After attending for a few weeks, she connected with some women who took an interest in her life, and Kanak became involved with them as well. Their company was both exciting and helpful, and the ideas they shared seemed to work, at least to some extent. Kanak found some satisfaction in a few of their suggestions, recognizing that something was better than nothing. After the sessions, her friends would linger, and Kanak would join them as they visited local restaurants and vented about their husbands. However, she kept her own issues with Samrat more private, revealing only to a certain degree.

"My husband used to stay out so many times. And I never minded that until I found him with a girl," one of them shared during the counseling session.

"When I caught him red-handed, I didn't react too much, which, of course, aggravated him and made him feel guilty for his actions," she continued.

Kanak was amazed by the idea and thought of implementing it, but she decided to omit the suspicion because she trusted Samrat completely however she thought *'ignorance is bliss'*.

On one of the same nights, Samrat didn't come home, instead, he called.

"Hey, sorry, but I'm staying at the department tonight..." he informed Kanak.

"Oh, no problem. Will you be coming home tomorrow morning?" Kanak asked politely. She didn't complain or argue, just accepting whatever Samrat had to say.

"Are you okay?" he sounded concerned.

"Of course. I understand now. I will keep your breakfast ready. Good night," she reassured him.

After ending the call, she breathed a sigh of relief, feeling like an actress who had given their best performance. With a grin, she went to her bed. Later that night, Samrat unexpectedly knocked on the door, and Kanak, who might have been dreaming, found Samrat inside the house. She woke up from her dream and covered herself with a shawl from the floor.

Confused, she asked, "How did you get inside?"

"I still live here, honey. I knocked, though," he replied.

"Am I dreaming?" Kanak wondered aloud.

"Of me?" Samrat teased.

"Yeah, sure."

Hiding her smile with her hand, she sat across from him and poured him a glass of water. Smiling to herself, she gazed at her husband, feeling content that she had accomplished something significant. On the other side, Samrat was unaware of her intentions as he enjoyed his supper, catching her gaze from time to time.

"What?" Samrat asked, his expression filled with doubt.

"It's been a while since I've seen you having dinner," she said, sliding a plate of salad towards him.

"Really?" he said.

"Last time was a month ago. It's been too long, I assume," she replied.

"Well, my job..." he tried to explain.

"Yeah, yeah, your job. Now eat up and come to bed," she said, urging him.

"Eat this salad too," she continued.

"Sure," he grinned.

Her tricks worked for a few days, but eventually, things returned to their usual pattern. Samrat resumed his past behavior of staying absent. He would leave the house early and only return to change clothes and eat food. Kanak's initial joy vanished, and she realized that Samrat was not going to change. It seemed she didn't need to care more or less for him.

However, things took a small turn when Samrat started spending nights with his wife. At first, Kanak was perplexed, thinking that she had tricked Samrat into staying, but the past few weeks had been different. She hadn't used any tricks; it was Samrat himself who chose to stay. He returned home after investigating the lady's apartment, and Kanak, who was out for groceries. She had started preparing a special supper for him these days. As he poured wine to distract his thoughts, Kanak returned home with her groceries and took the same glass of water that Samrat was drinking.

"You have started spending your nights with me." She said before sipping.

"You don't want me around?" he asked.

"I didn't say so."

"I don't know. I had this call from a lady. She was strange. At first, she said she saw a murder happening but then she refused to accept it. And later she mentioned one more murder that she saw from her bedroom window."

"It's fascinating" she continued

"She remembers the murders. Or maybe it was her mistake."

"Maybe. But I'm not following her statements. She made a call about the murder, when I reached her apartment she didn't mention any crime, it was like she forgot why she called me for."

"What did you do?"

"Well, I checked her apartment, and nothing suspicious."

He took out the scrambled paper that he brought from Ahilya's house.

"Just this. But later when I left her house she screamed about the murder, of course, I checked but nothing was there to report. And again, when I went back to her apartment she completely forgot everything she mentioned instead she mentioned a new piece of interest."

"What was that?"

"She mentioned that she saw a murder, days ago, in the same apartment, opposite her building."

"She has Amnesia, I guess. Did she report about it or did she again forget?"

"She said she reported the incident but persistently she can't remember what happened next. However, she took a note of it."

"Note of it? Okay."

She grabbed his hand slowly and gave a peck on his fingers. Samrat smiled a little and then drank all the water left in the glass.

"Don't drink too much. Leave some space for dinner." She commanded in a wife-like manner.

Samrat playfully held her wrist and smirked, pulling her closer to him. He whispered in her ear, "Are you sure?" Kanak nodded in agreement, took the glass from his hand, and put the bottle back in its place, then started preparing dinner.

After their dinner, they were ready to sleep except for Kanak who had planned on something else. It was a busy day for Samrat, according to himself. He wanted to rest and give his mind some peace. On the contrary, Kanak wanted to make him stay awake and spend some time watching TV together.

"Shall we watch TV? It's been a while." She requested more like a demand.

Samrat, determined to sleep, tried to ignore her. Kanak continued, voicing her concerns about his attitude and negligence.

"Samrat?"

"Baby, not today, please. I am so not in the mood to discuss this," Samrat said, half-asleep.

He was trying to sleep by passing over her question.

"Why do you act like this?" she argued.

"Act like what?" Samrat asked, his eyes still closed. He was all set to fall asleep but Kanak's voice kept him awake.

"You know I'm trying to settle in with you. Your attitude, your negligence..."

"Baby, not today, please. I am so not in a mood to discuss this."

"Oh! I'm sorry Officer Chauhan, did I commit any crime?"

"No, you didn't but I still want to punish you"

"Punish me?" she asked confusingly.

He wakes up from his half-sleep and grabs her waist.

"You are being a wifey nowadays"

"And what does that mean?"

"That means..." he kisses her neck and makes her fall on the bed.

"That means you are making me punish you." He continued.

"This is not what I asked for though,"

"Oh, you did. This is exactly what you asked for"

For a while, they continue to kiss each other sometimes on the neck or the lips. Usually, married couples tend to make love after their kisses but here nothing like that ensued. Not only Samrat but Kanak was too tired to make love with him. However, she got interested in the case mentioned before by Samrat.

"Samrat, one thought which couldn't escape from my mind is why did she call you? And how come she only remembers the murder?"

"I don't know."

"What did you do next?" she asked taking his hand and putting it under her neck. Samrat didn't give any answer. She asked again "What did you do then?" still no response which probably concluded to one response that he was asleep.

"You rarely discuss… not discuss, introduce your cases to me, and yet you never completely tell me about them," Kanak said. She too turned to his side and eventually fell asleep.

CHAPTER 3
THE LONG HOURS OF WAIT

"How was your fish?" Officer Rao asked as soon as he found Samrat. Samrat was less bothered to give him a reply instead he sat quietly on his seat taking out his diary from the pocket of his pants. He went to the page where he had jotted down the points from his previous investigation, that lady's apartment. Also, he had placed the scrambled papers inside that small diary. He placed them in front of him.

"Won't talk?" Officer Rao asked again.

"I am sort of busy here... Do you mind sneaking somewhere else?" Samrat replied.

"Can I have a look? I can be helpful too." Officer Rao suggested.

Samrat handed him his diary in a way that he shouldn't turn pages or check other scribblings he had done inside it.

"Careful."

"It's just a diary."

"For you."

Taking the diary from his hand Officer Rao acknowledged some of the notes Samrat had mentioned. It appeared to be familiar with him too. After reading the notes from the page, Rao tried to turn the page but Samrat soon took the diary from his hand.

"Enough for now."

"This lady, she's psycho I guess."

Samrat gave him an uncanny look. He didn't follow up on what Rao was trying to put.

"I have experienced her too. At first, she informs you about the murder in the apartment opposite to her building but when you arrive on the spot..."

"She acts as an absolute stranger." Samrat finished.

"Yeah!"

"It doesn't feel right, though," Samrat said.

"When did she report the crime?" he asked.

"A month ago, I don't recall. Maybe you can visit again at her apartment."

"For what reason?"

"I don't know, you might find something."

He did consider what his colleague suggested but his hesitancy didn't approve. He craved confirmation of what precisely was happening around that apartment. So, he determined to put more stress on his brain and went through the notes again which he jotted down during the investigation. In his diary, he mentioned some of the things regarding the lady that read

1. Didn't recognize me the 2nd time.

2. Sticky notes on the refrigerator.

He circled the first one and started recollecting the incident.

'I don't remember any calls. Who are you? Is everything okay, officer?'

'She didn't recognize me the next time and why did she scream?' He thought leaning back on his chair. He was getting confused thinking more about the situation. But why would he care about her and what difference do these two things make, he underlined the sentences. Then he remembered what Officer Rao told him about the lady.

'I have experienced her too. At first, she informs you about the murder across her apartment but when you arrive on the spot...'

Also, he remembers Kanak's words about *'Amnesia'*.

Samrat comprehends one important thing out of these. He realized that if he went again to the lady's apartment she probably won't recognize him. It's because she keeps forgetting.

"She forgot who I am after some amount of time" he murmured.

"And she won't even hark back to the fact that we have met before." He continued.

He understood what his next attempt would be, and so he kept his diary in his pocket and left. He went straight to his car and started the car's engine. He seemed confident enough about his second chance, so he decided to not ruin his confidence with another person's meddling.

When Samrat reached the apartment, he rechecked the address. He looked in the side mirror to check if anyone was entering the building but he found no one. He opened his car's door and without giving a glance to anyone he went straight to the building. As he was about to reach Ahilya's apartment he saw a boy who was staring at the walls.

"Hello, Officer?" the boy said.

"Hello, do you reside in this building?" Samrat asked.

"Oh no, I don't live here. I live downstairs." He said.

"Okay. Will you excuse me?" Samrat stepped ahead and started moving towards the door.

"She's not around!" the boy exclaimed.

"Do you know where she went?" Samrat asked.

"How will I know, Officer?" the boy joked around and stood in front of Samrat. "I hope she remembers her apartment." He continued.

That boy seemed suspicious yet his looks were innocent. He didn't appear like a teenager though, more of his physic was similar to teens. His face looked shrunk, and his hands were thin but his eyes were bright and innocent.

Despite that boy mentioning the lady being away from her apartment, Samrat purposely went towards the apartment for confirmation. He pressed the doorbell and no one answered, he knocked on the door, and again no one answered.

"I told you, Officer?" the boy said with his crooked smile.

"What's your name?" Samrat asked.

"Maddy or Madhav. Whatever suits you." He said.

"Thanks, Maddy." Samrat greeted him by shaking his hand.

"Anytime, Officer." Maddy said, "I should leave now." He continued.

Samrat nodded and smiled at him.

After Maddy went out of the building, Samrat meanwhile was waiting for the lady to arrive. A couple of hours has been passed and Ahilya was not yet to be seen around. Samrat checked his watch. It was dark around. Checking his watch, he realized he had spent hours waiting for her but he was assured enough to not move away from that building. So, he went out of the building and sat inside his car.

It was past evening she hadn't appeared at her apartment yet. "Maybe she did forget her apartment. I think I will wait around."

Though he was inside his car, his mind was outside the building waiting for the lady to arrive. And he couldn't stay idle for more than this.

He wanted to use this opportunity. He remembered how he lost one of his cases because of his overlooked behavior.

It was the time when Samrat was asked to keep an eye on the suspect. He was supposed to stay around him and keep a watch on his every movement. Samrat was standing out of a café taking his parcel. Along with his parcel, he returned to his car. The moment he sat inside he received a call from the station. He clutched his steering wheel while listening. After the call hung up he went straight to the suspect's house, it was locked. Samrat got frustrated without any minute he rushed to his car, started the engine, and began roaming around the area in search of the suspect. Unfortunately, he couldn't find the suspect and returned to the station. Standing in front of his senior with head down in ignominy.

"I was just grabbing some food," Samrat said.

"Yeah! This is how we lost him. For your food!" his senior said.

"Can you be a little serious about your job? I am the one who has to answer the authorities." Officer continued.

That was the day Samrat resolved if he would be taking any case under his interest he won't disdain his image in front of anyone. Deeming his past circumstances, he got out of his car and straight headed to Ahilya's apartment. The door was still locked so he sat on the stairs waiting for the lady to arrive. A small bulb that wasn't much bright yet light enough to allow one to see vaguely. He laid his head on his knee wrapping his arms around his legs.

It was midnight, and Samrat was half asleep, trying to keep his eyes as wide as possible. Shaking his head, rubbing his eyes, in every possible attempt to keep himself awake. He checked his watch, this was the ninth time he had seen his watch after arriving at the place. There was no sign of Ahilya. He tried hard enough to stay awake but his eyes started shutting, and his yawning was now in a row after every couple of minutes. He laid his head on the wall taking the support he found comfort and slept off thereafter waiting for hours. Every attempt to stay awake seems triumphant but for a minute. At last, you cannot win against your sleep.

It was dark and he was sleeping laying his head on the wall. There was a presence of someone arriving at the apartment. The face was half-covered with a cloth, only eyes visible that too was not clear enough. Wearing a black overcoat, and holding shoes in hand which made it clear that he is a man. His steps were as quiet as possible as if the person didn't want to let anyone know. It appeared as if the person was waiting for Samrat to fall deeply into his sleep. The steps got closer to the apartment and Samrat. He opened the door and went inside, closing the door behind him as hushed as possible. It was someone unfamiliar, hiding their appearance, walking privately, it appeared that the person was concealing his presence and didn't want to disclose who it was.

A few minutes later, after him, someone else came around. It was pre-dawn, and a lady, covered in a black scarf, her face was masked and her eyes were covered by goggles. It was indeed uncanny that she appeared in that fashion. She walked past Samrat minding his presence. She was quiet so that Samrat couldn't hear her walk. Same as the other man. She crept and slowly opened the door of Ahilya's apartment and went inside. She closed the door softly and real hushedly as if she wanted not to let Samrat hear anything.

An hour later the man, same as before (covered) passed by Samrat, he first stood next to him, staring but then went off. After him, the same woman same as she appeared before, stood behind Samrat. Gradually she placed her hands on Samrat's shoulder, clenching it, she pushed him.

"Damn it!" Samrat shrieked.

His hand innately went to his gun but he didn't take it out. A nightmare he supposed, the worst one. He never had any such nightmares before. Though he was occupied with cases that involved various incidents that could trepidation him, however, he never had any such situation.

This first experience was a terror for him and it startled him. Without any ulterior thought, he went for the door. But the door was still locked and there occurred no signs of Ahilya. He was alerted now though waiting for her at this place appeared different now so he went out of the building and reached for his car. It was dawn with hardly any humans around. Before entering his car, he gave a glance at his watch, a digital one that showed '4:02'. It's quite early to investigate, or to ask people around about anything in these early hours, he thought. Despite this, he was determined to locate any clue, any fucking clue to lead this story of Ahilya. He sat inside his car, waiting for her.

CHAPTER 4
AN ATTEMPT

An hour later, Samrat remained seated inside his car, hoping for a glimpse of Ahilya. A vehicle pulled up near Ahilya's building, and Ahilya emerged from it. Samrat observed her movements intently, even though he considered it a futile endeavor to conduct an inquiry at such a late hour. Nevertheless, his determination kept him in place, and he anxiously awaited the passage of time.

More than unraveling the mystery surrounding Ahilya, Samrat's focus lay on the opportunity for personal gain and recognition within the police station. He yearned to solidify his reputation as an astute police officer, known for both solving cases and assisting the public. His thoughts revolved around the current case, particularly since it involved a murder. However, his musings were tinged with bias due to the old lady's apparent unawareness of her surroundings and actions. Was she truly a witness to a murder transpiring near her building, or was it merely a figment of her imagination? The presence of murder-related novels on her table planted seeds of doubt in Samrat's mind, causing him to reconsider his decision to reinvestigate the premises.

He waited patiently until the clock indicated a suitable time for investigation. At precisely 7:30 in the morning, the telephone at the police station rang. Constable Durgesh Patil, who was on the night shift, answered the call.

"Hello, Constable Dur..." the voice on the other end began.

"Hello, Officer. Please come quickly. There's a man covered in blood standing near my apartment building," the distressed caller informed.

Durgesh remained unfazed, knowing exactly to whom he should relay this information. After concluding the conversation, he dialed Samrat's number from his cellphone.

"Hello, sir. I received a call from that old lady at the station," Durgesh reported.

Samrat, half-asleep, answered the call.

"Who?" Samrat inquired.

"That old lady, sir—the one you've been investigating. She called again, at this hour. She claimed to have witnessed something, not a murder per se, but she mentioned a man covered in blood," Durgesh explained.

"Okay, thanks," Samrat replied, swiftly making up his mind.

He headed towards Ahilya's apartment without hesitation. Finding the door slightly open, he knocked and called out for her. She appeared at the door in a flustered manner.

"Yes," she responded, her voice filled with unease.

"I apologize for disturbing you at this hour, but I need to ask you a few questions about the call you made earlier," Samrat said.

"Yes, I hope you'll believe me. I truly saw someone covered in blood. I'll show you, please come in," Ahilya replied, opening the door wide to allow Samrat entry.

As he stepped into the apartment, he noticed a black scarf lying on the couch—a sight that triggered memories of his nightmare. Before he could approach the scarf, Ahilya called out from her bedroom.

"From this window, I saw him. I even told Madhav, but he refused to believe me," she exclaimed.

"Madhav?" Samrat questioned, intrigued by this new piece of information.

"My neighbor from the other floor. He's a good kid," Ahilya informed Samrat.

As Samrat made his way towards the mentioned apartment, where Ahilya claimed to have seen a man covered in blood, he was certain that there was nothing untoward happening on the premises. Samrat recognized the potential that Ahilya might not recall the details she had shared during their conversation. Consequently, he artfully devised an explanation, informing her that his team was currently in the vicinity she had referenced and assured her they would promptly launch an inquiry. Ahilya acquiesced to his assurance. However, he deftly redirected her attention toward other matters. Also, he needed a reason to thoroughly examine Ahilya's own apartment. Rather than dismissing Ahilya's account, he assured her that he would look into the incident further, even though he had no intention of doing so, given her fragile mental state. Exiting the bedroom, he asked Ahilya for a glass of water, using it as an excuse to buy some time away from her presence. He lightly touched the black scarf lying on the couch as he pondered his next move. Ahilya returned from the kitchen with the glass of water and found Samrat seated on the couch, holding one of the novels in his hand. The books remained in the same place as during his previous visit.

"Are these books worth reading?" Samrat inquired.

"They help kill the time. I'm actually working on a novel myself, although I often lose track," Ahilya replied.

"Are *you* not going to check that place?" she asked, handing him the glass of water.

"Yes," Samrat responded, taking the glass but not drinking from it.

He stood up and made his way back to the bedroom.

"So, you saw the man from here?" he questioned.

"Yes, right in front of that window. It was horrifying. We should help…" Ahilya explained.

"A dying person often needs help, ma'am," Samrat remarked.

While inquiring about the man, Samrat carefully observed his surroundings. Nothing seemed suspicious about the arrangement of items in the bedroom. A solitary bed, a table to the left with a lamp placed upon it—aside from these, the room was bare, devoid of any additional furniture, which was to be expected for an elderly woman living alone.

Upon leaving the room, Samrat noticed Ahilya's startled expression. She was clutching a kitchen knife in her hand. His instinct was to reach for his gun, but he resisted the urge when he noticed that Ahilya had the gas on and was washing vegetables in a basket. She had started preparing her breakfast. To pass the time, Samrat decided to pick up the novel he had seen earlier. As he flipped through its pages, he noticed several sections that were folded. Intrigued by the possibility that these folded pages might hold some clue, he asked Ahilya about the book.

"Can I borrow this one?" he inquired.

"Of course, but please return it," Ahilya replied.

"Oh yes, it won't be considered as evidence," Samrat acknowledged.

Taking the book with him, he thanked Ahilya and left her apartment. As he stepped outside, Ahilya reached out to him.

"Is there anything else I can help you with?" she asked.

"No, I'm just leaving for now. I may…" Samrat trailed off as if he had suddenly realized something.

"I should go. Thank you," he finally said.

Feeling disappointed that his visit to Ahilya's apartment had yielded no significant results after the long wait, Samrat left the building. He tossed the book onto the backseat of his car, contemplating its potential for providing clues. However, his primary concern was the black scarf around the dog's neck, which bore a striking resemblance to the one in his nightmare. Delving further into Ahilya's personal belongings seemed both intriguing and dangerous to him. At times, he dismissed Ahilya's case as nonsense, while at other times, he believed it could shed light on his otherwise bleak police career. He longed for an opportunity that could propel him forward and earn him admiration from others. Seeking some solace, he dialed Kanak's number before leaving. The phone rang, but there was no answer from her end. Starting the engine, he drove off, pondering the mysteries that lay ahead.

Instead of heading home, Samrat made his way to the police station. He approached Officer Rao's table, holding the book in his hand, and inquired about the presence of the uncertainty in Ahilya's apartment.

"When I investigated her house, I didn't find any suspicions in her apartment," Officer Rao confirmed.

"How many times have you visited?" Samrat asked.

"Only once," Rao replied.

"Also, did she ever mention a guy named Madhav?" Samrat inquired further.

"No," Rao responded, sounding confused.

"Did you find anything suspicious?" Rao asked.

"Maybe..." Samrat replied, his tone indicating there was something he had discovered.

"Do you need my help?" Rao offered.

"I'll ask when I need it. Thanks," Samrat replied, appreciating the gesture.

"Either way, you should look into this guy Madhav. He might be of assistance. You can thank me later, though," Rao suggested.

Samrat nodded in acknowledgment and left the police station. Without wasting any time, he made his way to his car. However, instead of getting inside, he decided to call Kanak.

"What's wrong with her..." he said, his voice filled with concern.

Getting into his car, he dialed Kanak's number once again and started the engine. This time, Kanak answered his call.

"What were you doing?" he asked.

"Are you concerned about me?" she playfully teased.

"Just answer my question without asking more questions, please," he requested.

"I was out for a walk. I knew you weren't going to come home anyway," she replied.

"I am actually on my way home now," he assured her.

"Do you want me to prepare breakfast for you?" she offered.

"Are you already at home?" he asked.

"Yes, I'm at home. Come over," she said.

Ending the call, he accelerated his car, eager to reach home as soon as possible.

When he arrived home, clutching the book in his hand, he found Kanak in the kitchen, busy preparing breakfast. As he approached, she called out to him without turning around.

"Please don't come near me. Go straight to the bathroom," she instructed.

Samrat followed her command, heading to the bathroom. After freshening up, he returned to find breakfast laid out on the table, with Kanak seated on the chair. He pulled up a chair and sat next to her.

"I have a job for you that might pique your interest," he began, taking a bite of food.

"My interest?" she inquired, intrigued by his proposal.

"It's a novel I brought from that lady's home, and it's not considered official evidence. Her case isn't officially recognized," Samrat explained.

"Did you stay there all night?" Kanak asked.

"Yes, and I had a very unsettling dream. But before discussing that, I want to show you this book," Samrat replied.

He retrieved the novel, while Kanak continued with her meal. Returning with the book in hand, he placed it in front of her. Kanak gently touched the cover of the book.

"Forgotten Killings. Doesn't seem very intriguing," she remarked.

"How would you know? Have you read it?" he inquired, taking a seat across from her.

Kanak's response, avoiding a direct answer, raised suspicion. Instead, she questioned him about how he obtained the book. She refrained from touching it any further.

"I simply asked her for it. However, she insisted that I return it soon, so you have limited time to finish it," Samrat explained.

"As if she will remember about it" Kanak smirked.

"What?" Samrat asked confusedly.

"Nothing." She replied attentively.

"But why do I have to read it? Will it be helpful?" Kanak asked.

"That remains to be seen. Once you read it, you might uncover something suspicious," Samrat replied.

"I feel like you forgot to give me a thorough explanation. How will I distinguish between what's suspicious and what's normal? How can I draw any conclusions?" Kanak expressed her concerns.

"It's quite a headache," Samrat murmured.

"The rest of what I mentioned earlier is the complete story, except for one additional character that came to light today," Samrat continued.

"His name is Madhav, and I met him yesterday," he added.

Upon encountering the name Madhav, Kanak exhibited a subtle surprise, as though the name had previously been mentioned to her. Before Samrat could notice she fixed her expression.

"You've met him?" Kanak asked.

"Yes, when I went to her apartment, a boy who identified himself as Madhav was sitting on the building's stairs," Samrat explained.

"He seems to be aware of her condition. I'm going to question him further. But I also want to search for any clues in this novel, as every time I visited her apartment, this book was always separate from the others on the table," Samrat elaborated.

"Oh. So that lady doesn't have anyone at home? No relatives to take care of her? It's concerning that she's living alone in this condition. Have you tried contacting her family?" Kanak inquired.

"I thought about it, but I don't believe any harm will come to her while I'm around," Samrat reassured her.

"But you can't be there all the time," Kanak pointed out.

"I'll make the call now. Can you please focus on this task?" Samrat insisted.

Kanak nodded and took the book in her hand.

"I'll handle this; you take care of Madhav," she said.

"Sure," Samrat agreed.

"Will you stay? Should I prepare lunch for you?" Kanak asked.

"Not sure," Samrat replied.

"Okay, I'll take that as a yes. How about you rest for a while, and I'll do the reading?" Kanak suggested.

"Sounds even," Samrat agreed.

CHAPTER 5
THE AVOIDED PAST

Two single divan beds occupied separate corners of the room, which was noticeably small for two people to comfortably live in. Despite the limited space, each bed was designated for one person only. The room was shared by two college-going girls, both of whom were tenants. One of the girls followed a minimalistic approach, keeping only essential and useful items, while the other had a penchant for possessions, resulting in a cluttered corner. Each girl had her own distinct area within the room. One corner remained impeccably organized, with only the bare necessities, while the other exuded a vibrant atmosphere, adorned with floral décor and adorned with a collection of Polaroids stuck to the wall. Among the myriad Polaroids, Sakshi, one of the girls, intended to add another photo. Despite the wall already being filled, she diligently searched for a spot to accommodate the new addition. It appeared to be a challenging decision for her, contemplating whether to replace an old photo with a new one.

The landlord, known for her strict discipline, emphasized the importance of maintaining clean walls. Her objective was to have the room fully furnished for the next tenant as soon as the current tenant departed. In direct opposition to the landlord's rules, Sakshi defiantly stuck her Polaroid on the wall. This action sparked a dispute between them, resulting in a warning from the landlord regarding the violation.

The landlord lady's voice reverberated with frustration as she exclaimed, "I warned you not to damage my property, but you chose to ignore my instructions anyway."

Sakshi, in an attempt to reason, pleaded, "I'm only sticking them on the wall. Please allow me this one request. I promise not to do anything else like this again."

The landlord lady's stern tone persisted as she responded, "If I catch you disregarding my rules again, I will have no choice but to evict you from this place."

Despite the landlord's disappointment with the already incurred damage, she cautioned Sakshi to refrain from such actions in the future. However, Sakshi's collection of Polaroids continued to grow, and she yearned to display them on the walls, creating a backdrop for memorable pictures. She searched for a suitable spot, while her 'acquaintance Kanak observed her actions.

"Let it go," Kanak suggested.

"This is driving me insane!" Sakshi exclaimed in frustration.

"I don't want to replace any of the existing photos... Kanak, please help me with this," Sakshi pleaded.

"No one will even remember this when we leave this place after completing our degrees," Kanak remarked.

"And if our landlord discovers the state of your side of the wall, it will be a mess," Kanak sighed.

"Replacing it would be so easy for you, as you don't have any friends apart from me, and we don't even have any photos together to put up on this wall," Sakshi said, expressing her frustration.

Kanak detached her phone from the charger, stowed her wallet in her bag, and positioned herself beside Sakshi. Giving her a comforting pat on the shoulder, she exited the room.

Kanak and Sakshi were classmates who had managed to secure a rented room together. The apartment consisted of two bedrooms, with Sakshi and Kanak occupying one while the landlady resided in the other. Although the room was rather cramped for them, the affordable rent and its proximity to their college left them with little choice. They agreed to share everything in the room except their beds.

Initially, both Kanak and Sakshi appreciated the space, but over time, Sakshi grew dissatisfied as her belongings multiplied. While Kanak still found the place pleasant, peaceful, and sophisticated, Sakshi found it increasingly confining.

'I wonder if you'll even notice my absence once I leave this place, Kanak. I just can't seem to fit in here.'

Sakshi would often express this sentiment whenever things didn't align with her preferred style. She and Kanak were quite different from each other, with distinct tastes and preferences. Sakshi, known for her friendliness, extroversion, and popularity among students (though not for her academic pursuits), had a pattern of having new boyfriends every two months. She would bring her male friends to the apartment whenever the landlord lady was away. Despite Kanak's repeated warnings, Sakshi never sought consent, fully aware that the response would likely be unfavorable. Kanak's admonitions ultimately fell on deaf ears, and she, too, grew apathetic towards such matters. Kanak's time was primarily occupied by college and her job, often returning to the apartment late at night. With no other place to go, she felt tethered to it.

In their class, Kanak remained relatively unknown and lacked popularity. Sakshi never introduced Kanak to any of her acquaintances, even though they shared a room. However, this lack of social connection did not bother Kanak, as she preferred a solitary life. They would exchange smiles, but that was the extent of their interaction. Kanak found solace in the company of books, predominantly fiction. Her preferred genre was crime, and she indulged in reading pieces that revolved around it.

On some evenings, Kanak and Sakshi would occasionally share a meal together, but Kanak would still find herself engrossed in her book. However, Sakshi had no intention of dining with Kanak due to her perception of Kanak as ignorant and rude. In turn, Kanak viewed Sakshi as loud and excessive. Both roommates chose not to eat together, except on rare occasions.

"Can we start eating?" Sakshi asked.

"Yeah," Kanak replied, flipping a page of her book.

"Seriously? Like this? It's a once-in-a-lifetime opportunity, and yet you're spending it like this?" Sakshi expressed her disappointment.

"We have this 'once-in-a-lifetime' opportunity every day in college, and you choose to spend it with your so-called friends," Kanak retorted.

"Okay, let's just ignore that and eat," Sakshi relented.

Kanak set her book aside and began to eat, while Sakshi picked up the book and started reading the cover page.

"You should become a detective. You always have at least one crime-related book with you," Sakshi commented with intrigue.

As Sakshi flipped the pages, the oil from her fingers left marks on the book. Kanak disliked it when Sakshi touched her book, but she restrained herself from reacting negatively.

"Is it interesting? Murders and crimes..." Sakshi continued.

"It depends. I find it interesting," Kanak replied.

"Have you seen a crime scene in real, is it good?" Sakshi asked excitedly.

"A crime is only fascinating when it is read as a story" Kanak replied.

"Our landlord lady also has novels like these. I sneaked into her room," Sakshi shared curiously.

"You should avoid sneaking into her room," Kanak suggested.

"Her room is plain, dull, and, of course, boring! But she has a good range of books, you can take one!" Sakshi suggested.

"I don't want to steal anyone's belongings. Maybe you should avoid it too, or else we might be evicted from this place," Kanak advised.

"And you told me to eat, and now we're having a discussion," Kanak remarked.

"Okay, fine," Sakshi acquiesced.

"But don't think you should become a detective. You're really into this stuff," Sakshi commented playfully.

"We make plans, and God laughs. Now, please continue your dinner," Kanak stated.

"What does that mean?" Sakshi asked.

"It means I don't want to delve into any further conversations about my future. And why all of a sudden are you so interested in me?" Kanak asked.

"Am I going to be your gossip topic for tomorrow in class?" Kanak continued.

"Just so you know, I don't gossip about you because your topics would only bore others. You... well, let's just say you're pretty dull, Kanak. So, don't promote yourself," Sakshi sarcastically retorted.

This became a common occurrence for them. Despite their numerous conversations, Sakshi never disclosed it because she had a soft spot for Kanak, who had helped her during her early days in college.

However, the reference made by Sakshi regarding Kanak and the landlord lady was indeed accurate. Kanak and the landlord lady shared similar tastes in almost everything. They were both avid readers, uninterested in the outside world, and unaffected by others' opinions. Nevertheless, they had no expectations from each other. The landlord lady refrained from pursuing any kind of relationship, likely due to past experiences, while Kanak had no desire to form attachments. Her sole focus was on her studies, and nothing else concerned her. The landlord lady, too, avoided any connections that might bring her closer to Kanak. She harbored a fear, something she had lost in the past due to becoming attached to an outsider.

"You two must be related," Sakshi remarked to Kanak while they were in their room.

"Kanak, you barely speak to her, yet she seems fond of you. Why?" Sakshi inquired curiously.

"It's probably because I keep her walls clean," Kanak joked.

"Well, when I leave this place, you two can enjoy each other's company," Sakshi commented.

"Have you found a new place?" Kanak asked.

"Oh, I'm sorry, Kanak, I forgot to mention it. I'll be moving next week," Sakshi responded.

"Where to?" Kanak inquired.

"It's just five minutes away from our college," Sakshi revealed.

"Will you be living alone?" Kanak questioned.

"No, I'll have a roommate," Sakshi replied.

"Your boyfriend? You said you weren't serious about him, and now this sudden change in plans?" Kanak probed.

"He's not that bad," Sakshi defended.

"Well, if he's paying rent, then he must be pretty good," Kanak remarked with a hint of sarcasm.

When Sakshi made the decision to move elsewhere, it created a financial burden for Kanak, as she had to cover both her rent and college expenses. While Kanak worked part-time to manage her personal expenses, her father took care of her college fees. Having Sakshi as a roommate helped ease the load, as they split the rent in half. However, even with her part-time job, paying the full rent remained a challenge for Kanak. She approached her landlord and proposed paying the rent in smaller installments. The landlord agreed to the arrangement, with Kanak paying eighty percent of the rent and assisting with household chores. Kanak accepted the deal and began dedicating a significant amount of her time to tasks like laundry, dishes, and cleaning.

One day, when the landlord found Kanak in tears, while she was washing the utensils, the landlord lady felt sorry for her and unexpectedly offered to alleviate some of her burden. She allowed Kanak to stay in the apartment rent-free until she finished college. Initially, Kanak hesitated to accept such a significant favor, but she had no choice as the landlord gave her an ultimatum: either live there rent-free or leave. Kanak ultimately decided to stay in the apartment without paying rent, which brought her a great sense of relief.

During vacations, Kanak would hardly visit her parents and even if she would she couldn't stay for long due to work commitments. However, living with the landlord lady proved convenient for her. One day, while preparing tea for herself, Kanak made an extra cup for her landlord.

"Hey, I made tea. Would you like some?" Kanak offered.

"Sure," the landlord lady replied.

Kanak had a habit of reading while enjoying her tea. If there was nothing to read, she would simply refuse the tea. After preparing the tea, Kanak handed a cup to the landlord lady and retreated to her room with her own cup. However, the landlord lady insisted that Kanak join her.

"But ma'am, I usually..." Kanak started to object.

"I know. Just sit with me," the landlord lady insisted.

Both of them quietly sipped their tea. When their cups were empty, the landlord lady handed Kanak a novel titled 'Forgotten Killings.'

"This is your last semester, and I know you won't be around after this. Giving you this farewell gift is unusual, but we share a common taste in reading," the landlord lady explained.

"How did you..." Kanak began to ask.

"I noticed your room filled with such books. I know reading helps pass the time and provides solace. You read books to escape uncertainty around you, and I used to do the same," the landlord lady shared.

"You love reading crime stories, and so do I. This one is my favorite," she added.

As Kanak sat in the living room with the book, a perplexed expression crossed her face. Although she had evaded Samrat's question, she knew he wouldn't forget about it. Flipping to the first page, she began reading. The story didn't intrigue her as she already knew it, but a disturbing feeling stirred within her, and she tried to maintain inner peace.

Kanak kept turning the pages of the book until she sensed Samrat approaching. He stood behind her, tucking his shirt.

"Which chapter are you on, baby?" he asked.

Instead of answering, Kanak questioned him, "What's her name? The lady you mentioned, the one who gave you this book."

"I never mentioned her name. Oh, she's Ahilya... Ahilya Mathur," Samrat responded.

Upon hearing these words, Kanak felt agitated. She closed her eyes briefly before turning to face Samrat, fully aware of how he would react if he perceived her state. Opening her eyes, she presented him with a radiant charm.

"I'm currently on chapter two, and if you think I can finish this thick book in just one day, Mr. Officer, I have other tasks to attend to as well," Kanak remarked.

"Alright, but please, baby, try to finish it within a week," Samrat requested.

"Are you heading out? More work?" Kanak inquired.

"Yeah, you focus on the book," Samrat replied.

As she walked past him, clutching the book in her hand, Kanak asked, "Will you be home for dinner?"

"Probably..." he responded.

"Okay, I'm going. I'll call you and let you know about dinner," he stated.

Samrat left the house, leaving Kanak feeling fragile. She held the book close to her face and softly whispered, "Ahilya."

CHAPTER 6
THE UNKNOWN GIRL

Upon arriving at the police station, Samrat's sole desire was to avoid encountering Officer Rao. Scanning the premises, he discovered no trace of the officer's presence. Proceeding to his desk, he extracted his diary in search of potential clues that could shed light on Ahilya's predicament. Captivated by her case, he believed it held the potential for a significant criminal investigation. However, he opted to keep his methods and inquiries undisclosed to higher authorities, choosing to take the lead himself. Uncovering any fragment of evidence that could render this case substantial became a matter of utmost importance to him.

Two possible avenues for advancing his investigation presented themselves. Firstly, engaging in a casual conversation with Madhav, and secondly, personally visiting the scene of the crime. His primary focus centered on conversing with Madhav, the individual with a crooked smile. Nonetheless, before meeting him, he felt compelled to connect the dots from his diary entries. Noteworthy points included Ahilya Mathur's amnesia, her consistent mention of murder, the visibility of the murder location from Ahilya's bedroom, the recurring presence of a bloodied man, the peculiar exclusivity to men, the identity of this individual, and the significance of the black scarf.

He jotted all the possible points in his diary.

1. Ahilya Mathur – has amnesia, and talks about murder (every time)
2. The murder spot is visible from Ahilya's bedroom
3. It's always a man covered in blood... why only man? Who is he?
4. Maddy/Madhav?
5. Black scarf?

Among all the details, Samrat circled the fourth one, 'Maddy/Madhav?' Recognizing the conversation with Madhav as his top priority and the most promising avenue for shedding light on the matter, he grappled with the implications of forsaking other cases and singling out Ahilya's as significant. Such a course of action would undoubtedly invite discord with his superiors and jeopardize his standing and work. Nevertheless, his eagerness to unravel this mystery, without first notifying his seniors, remained steadfast. He yearned for someone to oversee his duties whenever he left the office without notice, a person who could provide a veil of camouflage. But who could that person be? Officer Rao? No, that option was unequivocally dismissed. So, who could offer their support? Samrat pondered for a while, consumed by his thoughts, completely oblivious to the ringing of his cell phone. After several rings, a constable interjected,

"Sir, your phone is ringing."

Startled, Samrat glanced at the constable, momentarily unaware of his words.

"What?" he responded.

"Your phone rang multiple times."

Samrat retrieved his phone and read the displayed name before dialing the number.

"Any information?" he inquired during the call.

From the opposite end came the voice of the man whom Samrat had enlisted to oversee the gathering of any information regarding Ahilya.

"Yes, there's a tea stall owner who also works as a part-time broker," the person on the other end relayed.

"And?" Samrat pressed.

"He might be able to provide you with some information." He responded.

With this lead in hand, Samrat found it impossible to resist meeting the tea stall owner. Before leaving the police station, he encountered a constable and requested a favor.

"If anyone inquires about my whereabouts, please inform them that I am at a crime scene."

The constable hesitated, but Samrat insisted, "If this excuse doesn't suffice, come up with any other plausible explanation. Please."

With that, he exited the police station.

Compelled by the discovery of a potential lead, Samrat yielded to his insatiable curiosity and hastened towards the tea stall, driven by the desire to acquire any crucial information that might propel the case down a fresh trajectory, offering a glimmer of insight into the enigmatic occurrences.

Guiding his car to a halt near the tea stall, Samrat stepped out and settled himself at one of the tables. Placing a casual order for a cup of tea, he surveyed his surroundings as the stall owner brought him his beverage.

"You don't seem like a local resident," remarked the stall owner.

"I'm not from around here," Samrat responded.

"I've been running this stall for the past decade. Are you in search of a place to live? I can assist you, but I'll need a commission," the stall owner suggested, accompanied by a sly grin.

"So, this is your part-time job?" Samrat inquired.

"How can I survive solely on this stall? I have three children to raise. Are you interested in finding accommodation?" the stall owner persisted.

"Hey, stall owner, stop badgering him. Why must you hassle every customer who comes here for tea?" interjected one of the tea drinkers.

"He always does this... One day, no one will come to your stall for tea. Always so greedy... money-grubber," the person continued, voicing his frustration.

"That's alright, I understand how money plays a significant role in everyone's life. However, at the moment, my concerns lie elsewhere," Samrat calmly stated.

"Since you've been here for the past ten years, have you ever noticed a woman with long hair, average height, and a round face? She appears to be in her sixties," Samrat inquired of the stall owner.

"There are so many women around here who fit that description. Nowadays, it's hard to tell who's in their fifties or twenties," the stall owner jested.

"Do you have any photographs?" the stall owner asked.

"No, I don't. But have you ever encountered a woman with peculiar behavior at your stall? For instance, she might ask for tea one moment, only to forget why she came in the next?" Samrat probed further.

"Ah! You mean that woman," exclaimed the other person.

"Ahilya madam?" the person asked.

"Yes, Ahilya madam. Do you know her?" Samrat inquired.

"Yes, I collect garbage from her house. She's an eccentric woman, always behaving strangely," the person replied.

"Due to her struggle with memory lapses," the stall owner explained.

"She tends to forget things after a while, which leads to her behaving unusually." Samrat inquired further, seeking confirmation of the stall owner's familiarity with Ahilya.

"Indeed, she resides in a building just down this road's end. She arrived here about a month ago, and strangely enough, she doesn't retain any recollections." Samrat retrieved his diary and began jotting down key points, causing the tea stall owner to appear perplexed.

Curiosity getting the better of him, the stall owner approached Samrat and fixed his gaze upon him.

"Who are you? And why are you taking notes?" he inquired.

Samrat revealed his police identification and placed it before the stall owner's eyes, who, although unable to read it, comprehended its significance.

"I'm with the police," Samrat clarified.

"Apologies, sir," the stall owner promptly apologized, retreating to his original position.

"Please continue sharing what you find strange about her inability to remember anything," Samrat urged.

"Previously, she resided in the building directly opposite her current residence," the stall owner revealed.

"What?" Samrat responded, his astonishment evident.

Ceasing his note-taking, he fixated his gaze on the stall owner.

"She used to live in that building?" he questioned, seeking confirmation.

"Yes, sir. From her new apartment's bedroom, you can see the bedroom of her old apartment. I'm familiar with the place because I assisted her in renting that house," the stall owner disclosed.

"She has no recollection of her previous apartment, which is quite remarkable." The stall owner continued, sharing additional details.

"She was the owner of the entire building, sir. She used to reside alone in a two-bedroom house, so I helped her by finding tenants for the spare room. She typically preferred female tenants... I mean, it's understandable since she was a single woman, managing on her own..." he continued.

"When did she vacate her old building?" Samrat interrupted, seeking specific information.

"That remains unknown. It has been eight years since that night, the last time I remember, she was alone in the hospital, and after that, she simply

disappeared. Now, she has returned with a blank slate of memories, stall owner elaborated.

Samrat pressed for more information. "Anything else?"

"Yes, sir. Before leaving, she had two female tenants, both co students. They used to study at a nearby college, a rather prominent (the stall owner revealed.

Samrat probed further, asking about the tenants.

"Do you know them?" he questioned.

"No, sir. They seemed like outsiders, not from this city," the stall ov responded.

"And the college?" Samrat pursued.

"There's only one significant college nearby, K.M College," the owner informed.

Satisfied with the obtained information, Samrat stood up and caref stowed his diary in his pocket. He glanced around and offered a smil the stall owner.

"I trust you'll keep this information confidential. Furthermore, if ﹐ happen to observe anything unusual, please contact me," he instruc providing his contact number.

After acquiring the pertinent information, Samrat made the decisior visit Ahilya's residence, hoping to cross paths with Madhav. He stepp into his car, started the engine, and extended his hand out of the windo bidding the stall owner goodbye with a wave.

Upon reaching Ahilya's building, Samrat found himself unfamiliar w the precise location of Madhav's apartment. He positioned himself outsi the building, patiently waiting for someone to emerge so he could inqui about Madhav's whereabouts.

After a few minutes of fruitless waiting, his frustration mountin Samrat finally decided to enter the building. Much to his surprise, as h stepped inside, he caught sight of Madhav exiting his own apartment o the ground floor, situated directly beneath Ahilya's dwelling. Dressed in white shirt and dark grey pants, with an untied tie hanging loosely aroun his neck, Madhav hurriedly left the building, his gaze fixed upon the floo completely unaware of Samrat's presence.

"Are you in a hurry?" Samrat's voice startled Madhav.

"Oh! You frightened me," Madhav exclaimed.

"My apologies for that. Are you heading somewhere? Perhaps to work?" Samrat asked.

"At this hour? No, not to work. Actually... never mind. Why are you here? Did she contact you again?" Madhav questioned.

Madhav's incomplete response ignited a seed of doubt in Samrat's mind, yet he chose not to press for further clarification.

"No, I wanted to ask you a few questions about her. However, I'm afraid it's not possible at the moment, is it?" Samrat responded.

"You seem fixated on her, don't you? Is there something specific that has piqued your interest in your investigation, something that somehow connects to her?" Madhav inquired, his curiosity evident.

"Shall we find a more suitable location to have this conversation?" Samrat suggested.

"Is it merely a conversation or more of a cross-examination?" Madhav quipped.

"Perhaps closer to an interrogation," Samrat joked.

"I have thirty minutes to spare. Hopefully, that will be sufficient," Madhav agreed.

With Madhav's consent to engage in a conversation, Samrat gestured for him to take a seat in the car. Madhav walked towards the vehicle, his head down, and upon reaching it, he allowed Samrat to open the door for him. They both settled inside the car and once the engine was started, Samrat smiled at Madhav and inquired about a suitable place for their discussion.

"There's a small café near the corner of the road," Madhav suggested.

"Alright, let's head there," Samrat agreed.

And so, they embarked on the drive toward the café, ready to delve deeper into their conversation.

Reaching the café Madhav and Samrat took their seats across from each other. Samrat opted for a cold coffee, and Madhav followed suit, signaling the waiter to take their order and leaving a momentary silence between them. Madhav, seemingly distant, fiddled with his tie while Samrat quietly observed him.

"How long have you known Mrs. Mathur?" Samrat inquired as soon as he noticed Madhav finishing his tie.

"This feels like an interrogation..." Madhav began in a light-hearted tone but was promptly interrupted by Samrat.

"I don't have time for games. I believe it's in your best interest to cooperate, considering Mrs. Mathur's perplexing and concerning condition."

The waiter arrived with their drinks and placed them on the table. Madhav thanked the waiter while Samrat offered a faint smile. Once the waiter departed, they resumed their conversation.

"Since when do police officers show concern? Are you one of the good ones?" Madhav chuckled.

"It seems you harbor some resentment towards people like me," Samrat remarked.

Madhav traced the rim of his coffee glass with the tip of his index finger, his gaze fixed downward, and softly mumbled, "Well, perhaps."

"I assume I'm not mistaken in that regard. Care to elaborate on your reasons?" Samrat pressed on.

Lifting his head to meet Samrat's gaze, Madhav quickly averted his eyes and began scanning the surroundings.

"That old woman who constantly pesters you is my foster mother. She became a widow when I was young. Despite having enough means to support me, my mother and I decided to relocate here fourteen years ago. We wanted a fresh start, so we purchased a house and converted it into a two-story building. As you can see, I may look like a teenager, but I'm not. My appearance became a subject of ridicule, so I resolved to study and move away from this place once I finished my college years. However, that wasn't the sole reason for my departure. My mother became overly possessive. Her care morphed into suspicion. She started snooping around my personal belongings, invading my privacy. It became suffocating being around her," Madhav explained.

"So, you left, leaving her alone," Samrat concluded.

"Yes, I regret taking that step. We had an argument, and I left the house, staying away for about 2-3 years. But then one day, I decided to visit her. When I arrived home, I discovered she had two tenants living with her, two girls. I didn't inquire much about it. And later on, I encountered her again in the hospital."

"In the hospital?" Samrat inquired.

"Yes, that's right. When I saw her after my absence, she warned me not to come to that place. So, I refrained from visiting. However, one night, I received a call from one of her tenants. She informed me about my mother's accident, where she slipped in the bathroom and suffered a head injury from the bathtub or something. Upon reaching the hospital, I found my mother transformed into a completely different person. She didn't recognize me, refused to go home with me, and couldn't recall the name she had given me herself."

"Who was the girl who called you?" Samrat probed.

"I tried to contact her, seeking her information. I even approached the police for assistance, but they dismissed my request, saying, 'Jaa kar budhi maa ko dekh kya faltu ke chakkar me laga hai?' (Take care of your old mother, why are you bothering around?)"

"Yet, she did help you by informing you about your mother's condition," Samrat acknowledged.

"She mentioned that my mother had been injured by a bathtub, but she never owned one. She never agreed to buy it. Furthermore, when I arrived at the hospital, the nurse informed me that she had been admitted for the past month. The girl who informed me called me from my mother's phone."

"Why didn't she call you earlier? It seems like that girl is hiding something," Samrat speculated.

"Since my mother refused to recognize me, I started living in the apartment below hers. We used to reside in the same apartment where my mother now claims to see a man covered in blood. I don't know what happened with our house. I have no idea who that girl was... I want to uncover every detail because it's becoming unbearably painful for me to witness and hear my mother screaming suddenly, pointing at the window from her bedroom and shouting, 'He is covered in blood!' What's even more devastating is that no one in this neighborhood seems to know anything about her. Even the tea stall owner, who claims to have lived here for over 10 years, has no clue."

"My focus is fixed on that girl who called you," Samrat remarked.

"I'm sharing all this with you because you appear genuinely interested in this case. I hope I won't regret divulging all this information to you," Madhav expressed.

"I paid her a visit a few days ago. It's apparent she's been struggling with memory lapses," Samrat disclosed.

"Yes, that's one of the challenges," Madhav concurred.

"But I can't help but wonder, if her memory falters, why does she keep books in her apartment?" Samrat inquired, his curiosity piqued.

"That's a remnant from my mother. She was an avid reader, you see. Even though she can't recall much from her past, she still takes solace in reading. Those dog-eared pages you noticed? She reads and then, in time, forgets the tale," Madhav explained.

"Ah, that must be quite the weight on her shoulders."

"You have no idea. Thank you for your understanding, officer," Madhav expressed, offering a gracious smile.

Samrat stood up, offering a smile, and shook hands with Madhav.

"Rest assured, I'm personally invested in this investigation," he assured him.

CHAPTER 7
THE POLICE DEPARTMENT

Stepping out of the café, Samrat felt a sense of satisfaction in how things were gradually falling into place, leaving a positive mark on his investigation. The Ahilya case had evolved from a mere random occurrence into a unique puzzle, one that he alone had uncovered. Discovering the apartment where Ahilya had resided with another girl made it evident that this girl held a crucial connection. Who was she? And why had she called Madhav? The pieces were still scattered, but progress had been made.

As Samrat ignited his car, he took a moment to glance back through the rear window, on the lookout for Madhav. Sure enough, Madhav emerged from the café, eyes fixed on Samrat as he hailed a taxi. The idea of tailing Madhav briefly flickered in Samrat's mind, but he dismissed it. Now wasn't the opportune moment. Instead, he contacted an associate and instructed them to shadow Madhav, extracting every pertinent detail about him.

"I'll send you the photo and his address shortly," he assured before driving away from the scene.

As he drove, Samrat's mind was still grappling with the information Madhav had shared about their move to the new location and Ahilya's cohabitation with tenants. The image of the mysterious girl lingered in his thoughts. Despite his best efforts to piece things together, he realized this was tied to Ahilya's past, with her delusions stemming from there. She wasn't randomly pointing out details; the challenge now was how to help her remember the events. Samrat had two leads to pursue in unraveling this mystery: Ahilya's previous apartment and the enigmatic girl. The latter remained elusive, leaving him with the apartment as his primary focus. He needed to find a way to gain access.

Lost in contemplation, he failed to notice his ringing phone. When he arrived at the Police Station, a constable stood outside, giving him a pointed look as though to signal he should brace himself before entering. Though Samrat couldn't quite grasp the meaning behind the gaze, he sensed the gravity of the situation. Stepping inside, he found his senior waiting, engrossed in conversation with Officer Rao. As Samrat approached, Officer

Rao gestured towards him, prompting the senior officer to rise from his chair, his expression one of barely contained anger.

"I've heard you're immersed in a case, Officer Chauhan."

"Yes, sir."

"Don't you believe we should be kept in the loop on that matter?"

"At the moment, sir, it doesn't seem that critical. I intended to inform the authorities once I had concrete evidence."

"Have you found any?"

"Not entirely, but I have uncovered some leads…"

"That's enough!"

"You seem rather fixated, almost obsessed with this case. Do you think others won't take notice? I had hoped you would put that case aside and focus on the immediate matters at hand, but it appears you're captivated by that woman's ramblings."

"She isn't speaking nonsense, sir."

"How can you be sure? Are you her legal representative?"

"No, sir. I apologize."

The senior officer approached Samrat.

"Look, I understand you're in pursuit of something. I've been in your shoes before and made some errors. I only ask that you proceed within certain parameters, not to rush matters."

"Yes, sir."

"This is your final warning. I don't want any complications stemming from your end, at the very least."

"Yes, sir."

Once the senior officer departed the police station, a hush fell over the area. Many assumed Samrat would emerge visibly upset, but he didn't react. Instead, a slight grin played across his face, initially small but gradually widening. It was akin to a teacher scolding a mischievous student, yet the reprimand seemed to have no effect. The constables nearby were puzzled by Samrat's demeanor, and finally, one of them broke the silence.

"Sir, are you alright? The senior officer was quite harsh with you." One of the constables asked.

"Yes, sir, don't dwell on it too much." The other one said.

Samrat returned to his desk, took a seat, and listened to them with that enigmatic grin still on his face. Then he remarked, "I'm not dwelling on it too much."

"But how did he find out about this?" he inquired.

"Anyway, I believe I'll put my case on hold and wait for things to settle down. What do you all think?"

The consensus was in agreement, except for Officer Rao.

"Are you satisfied now, Officer Rao?" Samrat asked a hint of sarcasm in his tone.

"I know what you're thinking. But unfortunately, it wasn't me."

"I'm not bothered."

The department remained tranquil for a while, with everyone engrossed in their tasks until a distressed woman entered, cradling a newborn in her arms. She wept inconsolably, struggling to hold her baby. Her sobs filled the police station, capturing everyone's attention. A female constable approached her, offering comfort, but the woman's tears continued. Since Officer Rao was away from the station, cases like this typically landed on Samrat's desk.

"First, please stop crying... I can't understand what you're saying."

She wiped her tears with her hands and gently laid her baby down on a chair. Samrat extended a glass of water, but she declined.

"Now, tell me what happened. Did your husband hurt you?"

"No, sir. I was in a mall when... when a teenager approached me and snatched my purse... I was holding my baby, thank God he's safe."

She broke into sobs once more.

"Please, stop crying... please."

Samrat spoke firmly, hoping to calm her. The woman, a little frightened, managed to suppress her tears.

"What was in your purse? Money? Jewelry?"

"Ten thousand rupees in cash... all gone, sir. Please help me... Please find that thief and make him return my money. I'm a poor person."

"Alright... alright... Can you describe his appearance? What was he wearing, his face, anything distinctive?"

She began to detail what the teenager looked like a white shirt, dark grey pants, and a tie around his neck. She mentioned that he appeared older in the face, but his body seemed like that of a teenager.

"Are you sure?"

"Yes, sir. And he was carrying a bag."

The woman's description aligned with one individual in Samrat's mind. However, he wasn't entirely sure of his instincts, so he asked again, and the response remained consistent.

"Where exactly were you when your purse was taken?"

"In the mall."

"Please be more specific... Where in the mall?"

"I was buying clothes for my child."

"Which shop?"

"I don't know the name of the shop. When I came out after buying clothes for my child, the snatcher came out of nowhere and took my purse."

"What was the name of the mall?"

"Kolam."

"Alright, we'll look into the matter."

"But sir, you haven't written..."

"Don't instruct me. I said I'll look into it."

The woman nodded, gathered her child, and left the police station. After she departed, Samrat sighed and began to scratch his head. He had an inkling of who she was referring to, but he couldn't fathom why he would commit such an act. On the other hand, perhaps the person he suspected wasn't responsible; maybe there was another individual who snatched her purse.

Maybe.

Next, Samrat instructed one of the constables to visit the mall and review the CCTV footage from all the children's shops. This type of case was often overlooked, but something about it caught Samrat's attention.

"Didn't you complain about it to the people in the mall?" Samrat inquired.

"The security did look around but they could not find anything. Also, they wanted to keep me silent as the fame of the mall might be lost. Please sir look into this."

After listening to that woman's complaint, Samrat assured her that he would take care of it. Meanwhile, he dialed Kanak's number.

"Hey, what are you up to?"

"I'm reading that book. It's taking a while."

"I didn't ask about that. I mentioned I'll be home early, so prepare a nice dinner."

"Why? I mean, why early?"

"Well, there's nothing much to do at work, so I thought I'd join you after my shift."

"Alright."

He ended the call, preferring brevity in his conversations when he was out. Besides, lengthy phone discussions were never Kanak's preference. They typically focused on the essentials before concluding the call.

A few hours later, a constable returned from Kolam Mall, approaching Samrat with a mobile phone in hand. Officer Rao, who had just arrived home from work, stood outside the police station and observed the constable's hurried approach. He couldn't help but wonder why the constable was in such a rush.

"Hey, what's going on?"

"Nothing, sir. A woman came in, crying, claiming her purse was snatched. Chauhan sir requested evidence, so I..."

"For such a minor matter, why are you getting all worked up?"

The constable smiled and entered the police station. Inside, Samrat was waiting for him.

"Any evidence?"

"Yes, sir. I checked the CCTV footage and had them send it to my WhatsApp. Here it is."

The constable unlocked his phone and played the footage. It showed the lady exiting the shop, and a thief snatched her purse, matching the description she had provided. However, the footage didn't reveal where the snatcher went after taking her purse.

"What about other footage? How can we catch him?"

"Sir, the camera didn't cover the entire corridor; only the front area was recorded. I also asked the owner of the adjacent shop, but his CCTV isn't functioning."

"Hmm."

"I believe he may have gone to the restroom and altered his appearance. But"

"Quite possible. But didn't people notice anything when he did that? It's not one man's job might others be involved in this? Alright... uh, you handle this case... See if we can enhance the quality of his image. I'm heading home."

"Understood, sir."

"If he had altered his appearance then it might be possible that a woman is involved with him. Anyway, keep me posted with this." Samrat mentioned as he left the station.

Samrat's queries about the description had been addressed. Even though the thief's face remained unclear, it was evident that he wasn't the person Samrat had suspected.

Upon reaching home, Samrat was greeted by the tantalizing aroma of cooking. He entered the kitchen to find Kanak preparing the salad, with the other dishes already prepared. He took a seat at the dining table and watched her.

"You're in a good mood. Did something positive happen?" she asked.

"Yes, something," he replied with a smile.

"Everything's ready... you just need to change and eat."

"Can I eat first and change later?"

"At least wash your hands, and I'll serve in the meantime."

Samrat washed his hands, returning to a set table.

"This looks delicious.."

He took his first bite and was instantly lost in the flavors.

"This is amazing... really amazing. Today is definitely one of my favorite days."

"And why is that?" Kanak asked, her face beginning to show signs of nervousness.

"Today, I found another lead in Ahilya's case. A strong one."

"What did you find?" Kanak asked her expression now visibly tense.

"I found her son. I've mentioned him before, but not as her son."

"Maybe."

"Also, I received a warning from my superior not to focus too much on that case, but..."

"Yeah... I mean, will it be worth it?"

"Of course, it's going to change our lives. Don't worry, everything is in order."

Kanak served herself and began eating slowly.

"Don't worry, I won't lose my job."

"Yeah. But don't you think... You've started sharing your work life with me. You never used to do that. After Ahilya's case, you've begun telling me things about your work and investigation."

"Yes, because you're a part of it."

The phrase *"You're a part of it"* sent a shiver down Kanak's spine, but she pretended not to be alarmed, as she couldn't afford to expose herself. It was something she had never wanted to be revealed, something from her past that haunted her, something she had concealed. She wiped the sweat from her forehead before Samrat could notice.

"How am I a part of it?"

"Because I had you read that novel given by her. How much have you read?"

Kanak breathed slowly, realizing that some things weren't meant to be shared.

"Yeah... It'll take me a week."

"Alright. The pages in the book were folded... did they mean anything?"

"No... not really."

They continued eating their meal, chatting, and reminiscing about their wedding days. However, Kanak couldn't shake off her unease, and Samrat's words, *'You're a part of it,'* kept echoing in her mind.

CHAPTER 8
THE BETRAYAL OF TRUST

Kanak had just four more months of her final exams before returning home. Her parents had already begun the search for a well-established groom who could provide a separate living arrangement for their daughter, sparing her from the pressures of traditional in-laws. While Kanak did have aspirations for a career after completing her studies, she rarely dwelled on these matters. That's why she was never inclined to return to her parents' house. She found solace here, a place where she could rest peacefully at night without the burden of unwanted parental expectations. Work became her refuge during vacations; even though she had free days, she avoided spending too much time with her parents, fearing it would drive her to madness.

One afternoon, on her way to work, she received a call from her father. She knew what he was going to say, so she braced herself.

"We've found a match for you. He's a few years older, with a job in the police force," her father stated, his tone more confirming than inquiring.

"In four months, I have my semester. Instead of wishing me luck, I get this," she sighed.

"Don't give me any more excuses this time," her father pressed.

"They're not excuses! I have to focus on my work," she exclaimed, hanging up the phone.

During her last vacation visit to her parents, they hadn't welcomed her with enthusiasm, still holding a grudge from their previous arguments over the phone. She was well aware of their strong belief that she should be married before turning thirty. When she arrived home, there was no warm reception, only a sense of bewilderment. Without exchanging greetings, she went to her room and began to unpack. She sighed and settled onto her bed, scrolling through her phone. A message from her landlady brought a faint smile to her face. Maybe it would have been better if she'd stayed, she mused, setting her phone aside and allowing herself a short nap.

In the adjacent room, her father was reprimanding her mother for not being attentive enough to their daughter. Their disagreements had become routine, stemming from every little inconvenience.

"If this is how she behaves, what's the point of all her education?" her father's voice echoed.

"Are we really asking for too much?" He raised his voice again, assuming Kanak might be listening.

"She's just arrived home. Can we let it pass for today?" her mother implored gently.

"Fine!" her father replied with a raised voice.

Kanak's impending marriage had become a source of stress for her father, and for Kanak, it felt like a constraining force. Her best strategy was to avoid their conversations or keep her distance from them altogether.

When she saw her dad's call, she reluctantly answered, knowing she couldn't avoid him for long. Conversations like these with her dad had become a regular occurrence, and she was growing accustomed to them. Setting aside her concerns, she hurried to work.

Apologizing for her tardiness, she quickly went to the cash counter. Fortunately, the owner was a kind-hearted man who understood the challenges his employees faced and never complained. Kanak, in turn, never took advantage of his generosity.

As the day grew darker, Kanak approached the owner with a request. With her exams approaching, she wanted to forgo her night shift to focus on her studies. She agreed to work until evening.

"No problem at all, Kanak," the owner reassured her.

"When are your exams?" he asked.

"Only four months are left," she replied with a somewhat melancholy smile.

"Don't worry, things will work out. And if you need anything, just let me know," he encouraged her.

Kanak packed up and left the shop. She contemplated calling Ahilya for groceries but decided to grab food from outside to avoid the hassle of cooking.

Upon arriving at the apartment, she rang the doorbell with a small smile, looking forward to helping Ahilya with arranging the dinner together. However, it wasn't Ahilya who opened the door. Instead, a man in his forties, disheveled and slightly intoxicated, greeted her with a smirk. Kanak was taken aback to find a stranger in such a state within the apartment. Without entering, she began questioning him. However, before she could get answers, he pulled her inside, gently covering her mouth, and began to laugh.

"You're early tonight. I thought you'd be out later," he commented.

Kanak pushed him away.

"Who are you? Why are you here? Where's Ahilya? How did you get inside?" she fired off questions without giving him a chance to respond.

"Who are you!" she exclaimed.

"Shh..." he hushed her, covering her mouth, and laughed.

"You're so loud. I wonder if you'd be better in bed."

Kanak was stunned by his words, taking a step back.

"Shut up!"

She rushed towards the door, but he pulled her back, pushing her onto the couch. He gripped her face, attempting to draw her closer, but Kanak kicked his leg, freeing herself. She pushed him away and seized the opportunity to flee to the kitchen. The man chuckled, then put a finger to his lips, signaling for her to be quiet.

"Shhh... don't shout."

And then he laughed again.

"You're strong, Kanak! You're strong."

He moved towards her, unsteady on his feet but determined. "I won't hurt you... please don't leave... I won't hurt you. I always wanted us to be together, you know... I like you so much, Kanak. I want to start a family with you."

"What?!" Kanak shouted.

"Shh... She'll hear you, and then she'll kill you... you know... jealous. She envies you... because I like you."

"Who are you?"

"She likes me... I like you... I don't like her..."

With a puzzled look, the man continued to confess his feelings to Kanak. She, on the other hand, was baffled by his behavior. He was a stranger she had never met before, and all she wanted was for him to leave.

"I've seen you leave this apartment many times. I always waited for you to leave. She told me to wait because she never wanted us to meet."

"Who?" Kanak asked.

"She always said, 'Wait for her to leave,' and I waited because... because... because she warned me."

"Who warned you?"

"See, she did something bad... see?"

The man staggered towards Ahilya's room, finding the door unlocked. He entered and began searching for something. The room was tidy and well-organized, with a stack of books placed near the bookshelf, already overflowing with books. He kept repeating 'photos' as he searched, indicating that he was looking for pictures. He pulled the bedsheet off, checked all the drawers, and even looked under the bed, but he couldn't find any photos. Growing frustrated, he began tossing things around the room in a fit of anger. In his rage, he shoved the bookshelf, causing it to crash to the ground, along with all the books. Some remained as they fell, while others sprawled open, revealing photos of girls. He picked up a few photos, laughing triumphantly.

He re-entered the main room, finding Kanak still stationed in the kitchen. Though she had the opportunity to slip away, curiosity held her in place. The persistent references to a certain woman had ignited a flurry of inquiries in her mind, and now she was determined to uncover the identity of this mysterious figure. While she considered the possibility of him leaving startled and dismayed, she also searched for something sharp she could use to defend herself. He didn't appear particularly strong, but he seemed capable enough to harm a woman.

Approaching slowly, he didn't notice that Kanak had a knife hidden behind her back. When he drew nearer, she discreetly concealed the knife.

He handed Kanak the photos. She hesitated, but eventually took them, her confusion turning to sudden shock when she saw images of girls - including herself.

"They still need to be priced" he laughed.

"What is this? Why were these photos in Ahilya's room?"

"Ahilya is a pimp. She preys on girls who are alone and makes them feel at ease. I told her to spare you, and she agreed," he explained with a smile, inching closer.

As he closed in, Kanak resisted, pushing him away when he tried to kiss her. He fell back, laughing scornfully.

"What are you doing, you wretch?"

"I saved you. I should be rewarded."

"Shut up!"

He got up, and with a sinister grin, approached Kanak again.

"Just one night, sweetie…"

"No!"

Kanak pushed him away and warned him to stay back. He persisted until he heard the sound of a knife falling from Kanak's back. Reacting quickly, she picked it up before he could reach it.

"Go away!"

"Fuck!"

"I said go away!"

"Bitch! Are you trying to kill me?"

He paid no heed to her warning and charged towards her to seize the knife. In her panic, Kanak brandished the knife, hoping to protect herself. He continued to advance, and in the struggle, his face was nicked by the knife.

"Damn!"

He stepped back.

"Alright, alright. Calm down. I'll move away from you and sit on that couch until Ahilya gets here," he conceded, retreating to the sofa.

"Leave my place immediately!"

"No… no… no…"

"Tonight, she's going to sell you. I'm just the delivery boy."

The words 'she's going to sell you' sent a surge of adrenaline through Kanak's veins, drowning out the man's words about Ahilya. The revelation that her photo had been taken and kept in Ahilya's room filled her with dread. Tears streamed down her face, but she fought to hold them back, along with the pain and disbelief. Her trust had been shattered.

"But why? You said you saved…"

"I won't!" he raged. But then in the next second, he calmed himself and said smilingly "Just kidding sweetie."

She wiped away her tears.

"How do you know her?" Kanak demanded, still clutching the knife.

"I'm not going to hurt you, girl. Just put that knife down" he said calmly giving a sense of assurance in his words.

Kanak took his words gently and decided to keep the knife before her proximity so that she could reach out to it as soon as he went bad.

"Who are you?"

"I'm a stranger, okay? You don't need to know my identity."

"Why are you here like this? What... what is all of this? These photos?"

"Ahilya is involved in illegal activities, she arranges and trafficks girls like you, and she called me!"

"No!"

"Fine! Don't believe me."

He took out his phone, unlocked it, and displayed explicit photos of him and Ahilya. He held the phone in front of Kanak, but the images were not entirely clear. Kanak moved closer to get a better look.

"I won't hurt you..."

For a moment, Kanak considered believing him and approached the phone cautiously. She took the phone from his hand.

"This can't be true... She's not like this..."

"Oh, then who is it? You?"

"No!"

In a room fraught with tension, the man settled onto the couch, relishing Kanak's struggle to come to terms with her predicament. She grappled with the stark reality, resisting its impact like a barrage of relentless needles.

"It seems she guarded her identity well."

"Shut up, you wretch!"

"Dare you!"

His wrath erupted, seizing Kanak by the waist and hurling her onto the couch. The phone in her hand met her face, leaving a small cut on her lips. Her attempts to resist were futile as he violated her, rending her shirt. She wept and pleaded, but his assault persisted until she recalled a pin in her back pocket, a memento from a previous customer.

With determined effort, she retrieved the pin and thrust it into his eyes. Blood streamed down his face, and he recoiled, shielding his eyes. Kanak seized the opportunity, maneuvering out of his grasp. She continued to fend him off with the pin until he struck her, sending her sprawling. Her lips bled from the forceful blow, leaving her bewildered and desperate for a solution.

Recalling a knife on the table, she began to crawl toward the kitchen. He, still in pain, thwarted her progress, sending objects cascading onto her legs. Despite the pain, Kanak persisted. When he again intervened, she stood her ground, her resolve unyielding. Again, she jabbed at his hand with the pin until he fell to the ground.

In the kitchen, she seized the knife, poised to defend herself. He lunged, seizing her hand, the knife still clutched within. Their struggle reached an impasse, his grip unrelenting. With her free hand, she gouged at his eyes with her thumb. He cried out, releasing her hand, and shoved her away. Infuriated, he sought to end her life. He seized her hair, slamming her head against the ground, then wrested the knife from her hand. Though blood flowed from her head wound, Kanak summoned every ounce of her strength. She overpowered him, sending him sprawling onto his back, where she swiftly ended his life by slicing his neck with the help of the knife.

The room bore witness to the grim aftermath, the floor stained with a pool of blood. Kanak, trembling and stained, held the knife, her gaze fixed on the lifeless body. She lay beside it, numb and detached, grappling with the enormity of her actions. Her thoughts coalesced around one desperate truth—she had acted to protect herself.

Unaware of the tumultuous events in her apartment, Ahilya raced toward the scene, her phone clutched tightly. Dialing a number, she waited impatiently, frustrated by the lack of an immediate answer. A second call, this time to Megha, offered little solace.

Reaching her apartment, she swung open the door, only to be met with a jarring sight. Kanak lay beside the lifeless body of the men, knife in hand, the room disarray of blood and strewn objects. Ahilya's heart raced, but her face bore no visible emotion. Without a second thought, she moved past Kanak, fixated on the lifeless man. Her foot met a pool of blood, staining her sandal as she pressed on. Shocked to find the man was the same person she had called moments ago, her forehead glistened with sweat. Her expression betrayed no tears, only a deep-seated dismay. She knew her attempts to rouse him were futile, but she persisted, hoping against hope that he might somehow respond, though she knew he would never again grace her counter.

"Lalit... wake up! What have you done, Kanak?"

She strained to shift his lifeless form.

"Lalit, what... in the hell!"

"He was misbehaving... I had to fight back..."

Kanak's words erupted, as though she had been rehearsing them silently, finally breaking the silence.

"You killed him! He was my most cherished client!"

Ahilya's voice was sharp, her disbelief palpable. Kanak's tears had ceased, replaced by a stunned silence. Ahilya's patience was already spent. Swiftly, she struck Kanak, wrenching her head in the direction of Lalit's body. This man had been pivotal to her, and now he lay dead. What explanation could she possibly offer to those who knew him? Another resounding slap sent Kanak off balance, trembling.

"I told you, I was trying to protect myself!"

"Shut up!"

"You—"

Kanak stood her ground, dropping the knife near Lalit's body. She wiped her face and yelled, "I said I was trying to save myself!"

"And look at what you've become!" Ahilya retorted.

Ignoring Kanak's protests, Ahilya retrieved the knife, brandishing it with fury.

"You bitch! He was a vital client!"

Rage clouded Ahilya's judgment. Revenge surged through her, a twisted form of greed that placed money above all else. This wasn't the landlady Kanak once admired; the revelation shattered her perception of Ahilya. Still, Kanak clung to the hope that she might hear the truth from Ahilya herself. Nothing else mattered but Ahilya.

"Who are you, Ahilya!" Kanak's voice reverberated.

"And who was he? He showed me... photos of girls from your room," she interrogated.

"Forget that! Why did you kill him, Kanak!" Ahilya advanced with the knife.

"I loved him with all my heart. He said he cared for you and never wanted me to harm you. But you... you harmed him. Why did you kill him?" She continued.

"I didn't! I was trying to—"

"To save? Since when does killing become saving?" Ahilya demanded.

"I treated you well, thinking we were kindred spirits," Kanak pleaded.

"What did you think of me? Just a means to an end for money?" Kanak scoffed.

"Why?" she screamed.

"I was playing a game... it's what I do, I deceive people, especially girls like you," Ahilya confessed.

"But you... you didn't just deceive me..." Kanak interrupted her, "Deceive doesn't suit you... it's not..."

"You're talking too much..."

"You took away my livelihood, my cherished client, my love."

"I did not kill him! I didn't!" Kanak stepped back, nearly reaching the door.

Ahilya lunged, the knife striking her. The weapon clattered to the ground. Kanak wailed and crumpled.

"When you die, you die alone," Ahilya declared, lifting the knife once more.

Despite her dazed state, Kanak resisted. She refused to beg for escape, for forgiveness. She believed in her own innocence, in her right to defend herself. Struggling, she delivered a fierce slap, dislodging Ahilya. With a surge of strength, she pushed her away, creating distance between herself and the blade.

CHAPTER 9
THE COMPROMISE

After conversing with Samrat, Madhav headed back to his apartment. Taking public transport, he reached his neighborhood, albeit being dropped off a bit away from his building. As he strolled home, a man in casual attire hailed him from behind. This man, bald with a round face and a somewhat mismatched mustache, was of average height, much like Madhav. Hearing his name, Madhav turned, recognizing the person, and waited for him to catch up. The man didn't sprint, but he walked briskly to save time.

"I've been trying to reach you," he mentioned.

Madhav retrieved his phone, checking for any missed calls. He spotted three from an unknown number labeled 'Information.'

"Haven't saved my number, have you?" the man quizzed.

Madhav locked his screen and returned his phone to his pocket, continuing on, the man keeping pace beside him.

"Any leads?" Madhav inquired.

"Not yet, but I did discover she was a student at a nearby college," the man responded.

"Anything more?" Madhav probed.

"I'll try contacting some college acquaintances," the man assured.

"Alright."

Upon arriving at Madhav's apartment, he swung the door open, offering the man a drink, but he declined and soon took his leave. Inside, Madhav found a note on the floor, reading 'Police Man was here again.' He closed the door, went to the kitchen, grabbed a chilled water bottle, downing its contents before tossing it aside. Returning to the living room, he settled onto the couch, phoning a number.

"I'm home."

After ending the call, he left the door ajar, seemingly awaiting someone's arrival. He returned to the couch, hearing footsteps nearing. It was Ahilya.

"Come in, Mom," he welcomed.

Ahilya joined him, and Madhav relaxed on the couch, finding solace in her presence. He rested his head in her lap, closing his eyes.

"Do you remember me?"

"I know you."

Despite Ahilya's struggle with memory, she always recognized Madhav.

"I've told him about us. He'll likely follow the leads I give him."

"What leads?"

"The ones that will lead us to the girl responsible for this."

"I'm not sure what you're talking about. Whatever it is, it must be for the best."

When Madhav first saw Ahilya in the hospital, he berated himself for leaving her alone. However, given the circumstances he uncovered, he couldn't have stayed with her earlier. He was twelve when Ahilya and her husband Ashok visited the foster care center, where they spotted him sitting alone, smiling. A small, fragile boy, and his tiny hair made him appear almost bald. Even though he was by himself, he seemed content. Ahilya was smitten upon seeing him, wishing to be his mother. They met the boy before departing, wanting to reassure him before taking him with them.

"Hey, how are you?" Ashok greeted.

"I'm good, uncle," the boy replied.

"What's your name, son?" he inquired again.

"My name is Madhav. Why?" the boy asked in return.

"We're thinking of taking you to your new home," Ahilya mentioned.

"You're our son now; we're going to be your parents," she continued.

"Is that okay with you?" she asked with uncertainty.

"I always prayed to God to send my parents to me... I won't be alone anymore," he said.

Madhav smiled, thinking that he was grateful that he now had them.

Eleven years had passed since he last saw her face after leaving her alone. She lay unconscious, her face swollen, and her hand bore fresh wounds. Though not too severe, Madhav worried about how she got them. Initially, he planned to stay a few days, and then return home, but her condition worsened, and he chose to stay, forever.

For the first few days, she was unconscious and heavily medicated. Madhav diligently fed her as instructed by the doctors. His concern for her grew, slowly erasing the resentment he harbored. The doctor had explained her diagnosis to Madhav.

"She'll keep forgetting things very often."

"How did this happen?"

The doctor clarified how the damage to her brain affected the limbic system, responsible for memory creation. He also explained the possible cause.

"Her head was injured when she was brought here. During the operation, the damage had already become severe."

"Will she get better?"

"Your mother has retrograde and anterograde amnesia. Patients with this condition struggle to recall past memories and have difficulty creating new ones. She may remember bits, but not everything."

As they talked, Madhav couldn't shake the thought of her head injury. He fixated on it but couldn't investigate it further at the moment.

When she regained consciousness at the hospital, she initially rejected Madhav, viewing him as a stranger. Nonetheless, he visited every day, and she gradually recognized him as a trustworthy figure. For months, he faithfully visited until the doctor discharged her. He brought her to his place, setting up an apartment for her on a different floor. He explained, "This is your new home."

"Thank you, son. You're helping me so much."

"Rest now."

Leaving her, he went to prepare dinner. Less than an hour later, he heard her scream. Rushing to her floor, he knocked on her door.

"Open up! Are you alright?"

Ahilya turned the knob, revealing a sudden wash of uncertainty on her face.

"What happened, Mom? Are you alright?" Madhav inquired, his concern palpable.

"I saw a man, covered in blood. He was... he was dead," she uttered, her voice trembling with fear.

"Where?" he pressed further.

"In that apartment... you can see it from my bedroom."

To verify Ahilya's claims, Madhav ventured to the building for inspection. The place bore the scars of a fierce blaze, its walls charred and devoid of any signs of habitation. Satisfied, he returned to Ahilya, ready to shed light on the situation.

"There's no one."

"Where? What are you doing here?"

He noted her demeanor and understood her condition. He supposed he should be prepared for these moments. Entering, he sat down on the couch with a weary smile.

"I just came to see you," he explained.

Taking a sticky note and pen, he asked her to sit beside him.

"I need you to do something for me. Given your unique condition, it would be helpful if you wrote down anything you think is important. Every time you do something significant, jot it down before you do it."

"Why?"

"Because I'm asking you to. It's not mandatory every time, only when you think it's crucial."

"Can you tell me why?"

"You tend to forget things, and it might cause problems if people find out."

He wrote, 'I forget things! So I have to write it down,' then headed to the kitchen. He affixed the note to the refrigerator before returning to her.

"Alright?"

"What if I forget to write?"

Madhav chuckled.

"Good question! Do you remember my name?"

"No."

"But you know I'm here, you acknowledge it."

"Yes."

"Likewise, once you start making notes and continue, you won't forget to make them anymore. It'll become automatic. And then you won't forget."

Madhav smiled.

"Will I ever get better?"

"You'll be okay..."

He refrained from calling her 'Mother.' Meanwhile, Ahilya gazed at the sticky notes, a touch of reluctance in her expression. She didn't want to agree, but she decided to do it for his peace of mind. Despite lacking memories of him, the bond between them held fast. To Madhav, she is still his mother, and to her, he felt like a son.

CHAPTER 10
GOOD AND BAD MEMORIES

Her interest in reading the book brought by Samrat was dull, she loathed reading any more chapters as she had already known how the story was going to end. And there was another reason as well that made her reluctant to do it. Despite being a bibliophile during her college days, her elation with books has vanished. Her loose enthusiasm was unknown to her husband who still believed that his wife was too engrossed in reading. It's because she never mentioned her lost enthusiasm to him, she kept away from him and however, and it was not the only thing that she avoided mentioning. There were things that Kanak enjoyed before being in a relationship with Samrat that somehow disappeared from her life and she circumvented them whenever Samrat asked about her past interest or likes. Keeping her things private she only mentions those particulars that she willed others to know. It wasn't like she was uneasy talking about everything with everyone, for her, it was something bothersome to tell her things, it certainly used to make her ignorant towards others, as she was never a person who was invested in others or was slightly interested in talking things out.

Being a private person, it was a favorable opportunity for her when she came to discover her husband's character and his tendency towards her. He too was someone who never really gave any potential to know what his wife was and what her early life was like before getting married. They were alike in some ways that made them closer to each other. For them minding each other's privacy was more important than forcing each other to open up.

Getting engaged to Samrat was not against her will, she made her choice, however, she needed some extra time with him before they got married. She wanted to fathom each other's perspective towards the relationship. And, Samrat too was convinced by her decision, yet it was not favorable to her parents to let their daughter wait for a year, they wanted her to get married soon to him as for them Samrat was a well-settled guy who would take care of their daughter. Also, he was the elder child of the family who owned a house which made him considered eligible for Kanak in the eyes of her parents.

Turning the page to the next chapter, she was clearly not attentive in reading, and the thoughts about her marriage and the days when she met Samrat for the first time were wandering in her mind. She continued to flip pages, her thoughts were strayed when she suddenly realized Samrat was in the house and waiting for her to finish the book in desire of getting some clue. She didn't finish the book nor did she have any shred of interest to finish, so she settled with lying to Samrat and telling him that she had completed the book and there was nothing that could make a lead through it. For some reason, she ought to tell Samrat to let go of the case of Ahilya, it was something that was killing her from the inside that suddenly her interest in everything was lacking. She no longer wanted to discuss what her husband had done regarding the case, nor did she ask him about it. And it was something that she refused to ever mention to her husband and yet again she chose to keep it restricted to him. Her past with Ahilya was something horrendous and mentioning this to her husband, a police officer was not an option for her. On top of that, Samrat was too involved in this case and she didn't want to break his trust by bringing up her past but this was something that would eventually be disclosed as Samrat by hook or by crook would surely make things out to reach to her past and he would find a right way even though she deflects him by something false.

She was in between the devil and the deep sea, however, she was robust towards her decision and the deed that she had done. For her it was not a crime, it was a defense and she had to take care of her then and now. While in her dilemma she forgets a brief about Samrat's presence and alarms when she finds his hand on her shoulder. He caresses her hair and slightly bends to keep his chin on her shoulder. Though being deeply involved in her thoughts she avoids her worry being expressed and slightly smiles to bring sophistication. She assumed that Samrat would ask her about the book and she was prepared to lie to him about her finishing the book, however this time it was an exceptional demand that he had proposed in front of her.

"I knew you would be surprised to hear this from me but I feel different today," said Samrat and sat next to her on the chair.

It was indeed bewilderment for her to find Samrat in this mood.

"I am so sorry for forcing you and making you a part of this greed. I know I am always busy and I don't pay attention to you and even when I am around you I still fail to be with you. And now all of a sudden I am forcing you to help me with my work and you with no question just doing it to make sure I make it out." He took her hand and gave a peck at it.

His face expressed his genuine love for her and it was so pure that Kanak couldn't resist her tears. She leaned towards him and kissed his cheek and all her notions were dissipated. A kind of relief was felt inside her heart when she kissed him, she felt sound around him.

"Why all of a sudden you are being too lovely to me?"

She smiled holding his hand tightly.

"I am always lovely to you it's just I don't express it,"

"We should go out together I want to take you out today."

She hesitated to say anything. And he was well aware of her answer. And before she could dispense with some excuse he shook his head in rejection.

"Do not say no because I am not at all asking you."

"Where will you take me?"

"To the moon?"

"Of course mister to the moon."

"I am not kidding, if we get drunk then we can surely go to the moon and I can make you drunk."

"You can make me do anything you want."

"Certainly."

She leaned closer to him she felt her heart race with anticipation, her lips beckoning him closer. And when their mouths met, it was as if time itself stood still. Though it wasn't their first kiss however, the delicate softness of her lips against his was like nothing he had ever experienced before a sweet and intoxicating sensation that left him longing for more and it felt to him as if he could continue this forever, he took what was adored at the moment and continued to kiss her. Her lips felt soft as cotton and he could not do anything but kiss them. They didn't even gasp. At that moment, they were lost in each other's embrace. It was as if they had been waiting for this moment and at last, it arrived. It was a long kiss.

After a while, they gazed into each other's eyes and she beamed at him, her illuminating smile was everything that Samrat had been savoring for that minute. She lifted his face with her gentle hands towards her and pressed her soft, tender lips against his skin. The warmth of her breath against his cheek overwhelmed him with the depth of the emotion and as she pulled herself away, still gazing into his eyes with adoration, he knew this was the moment he would remember for the rest of his life. And as Kanak's eyes dwelled on his face she couldn't resist leaving her place and sitting on his lap.

At that moment, she wanted to forget everything, every thought that had been eating her up from the inside, every worry that made her blood rush throughout her body. And when she pressed her body against him, in his embrace, she found solace from the chaos of her thoughts. All the worries and fears that had been haunting her disappeared as she nestled into his arms. The steady beat of his heart soothes her very soul. She wanted to feel sound around him, under his arms she wanted to be safe. She longed to forget all her troubles and lose herself in the comfort of his embrace. And as he found her completely lost in him, he held her close making her feel a sense of peace wash over her, a feeling of contentment that she had experienced after a very long time.

For a while, they held each other, when Samrat mildly moved her hand on her cheek.

"Get ready or I will change my mind for something else."

"We should stay like this forever. I don't want to leave this comfort."

"I am planning to take you to dinner."

"You are my dinner."

"Baby, get ready."

"Okay, okay."

When Kanak got up from him, she went straight to her bedroom and Samrat's eyes were gazing at her body from behind that looked perfect for him and he smirked thinking this was the woman he would never leave, and his ogling was broken by the voice of Kanak who from inside the bedroom asked him which shirt he will be wearing so that she could keep it out from the shelf. Without answering, he left his place and went to the bedroom where he found Kanak struggling in draping a sequined aqua-blue saree with an off-shoulder sequined black blouse. In that dress, she looked alluring. While draping her saree, she heard Samrat's footsteps reaching toward her and before she could make any attempt to hold her wife from behind and appreciate her look she commanded him to get ready without wasting any more seconds.

"Your shirt is on the bed along with the pants. If you waste any more time then I am changing my mind."

"Oh.. okay."

"This took my immense patient and I don't want you to ruin it."

"Understood ma'am. I'll be ready in a minute."

"Thank you!"

Before leaving their house, Kanak mentally ran through the list of tasks that needed to be completed before they left the house, Samrat patiently waited in the driver's seat. With his hand on the steering wheel, he watched her with a look of tender admiration, waiting for her to allow him to start the car. Despite the weight of her obligations, Kanak's focus never wavered, her mind running through each item on her mental checklist with precision and care. And as she finished, her eyes met Samrat's, a small smile of gratitude playing at the corners of her lips. With a nod of approval, she gave him the signal to start the car, and they drove off

"Everything is okay," Samrat assured while driving the car.

"You didn't tell me where we are going."

"It's just a restaurant, nothing special."

"Okay."

"I only wanted to take you out somewhere good."

"We could have stayed home, ordered some food, and…"

"No, no, and no."

"Fine."

"I was being cocky lately I am trying to be with you."

"You are such a sweetheart. Don't be sorry now. I don't mind you being out for work for long hours it's just sometimes I miss you and you are just not around. I understand your absence so I called you to just make sure you are okay but you don't even answer your phone. At least answer your phone when I call, that is all for me."

"I'm sorry."

"Let's just forget all that. I am happy today." She smiled and gently kissed his palm assuring him that everything was pleasant between them.

As they approached the restaurant, Kanak's visage conveyed her elation as she gazed upon it, leaving Samrat in no doubt as to how pleased she was with his choice of venue. Her flabbergasted face explained her contentment when she saw the restaurant and smiled at Samrat. Anticipating her reaction, he had carefully selected this establishment, well aware of the joy it would bring to his wife.

As Samrat parked the car, Kanak retrieved her purse and disembarked simultaneously Samrat too stepped out of the car and they held each other's hand before moving any step ahead. Upon entering the restaurant, a wave of nostalgic breeze washed over her as memories flooded back to their initial encounter before they were wed. As they took the seat, Kanak's eyes darted excitedly around the room, taking in every detail, while Samrat's gaze remained steadfastly fixed upon her. His decision to bring her to this particular establishment had clearly paid off, as evidenced when he realized how gleeful his wife was.

"It hasn't changed at all, Samrat," Kanak remarked.

"I know. I am so relieved to see you so delighted." Samrat replied.

"You remembered this place? Oh, my goodness! I've always wanted to come back here with you, you know!" Kanak exclaimed.

"I'm sorry it took me so long…" Samrat offered apologetically.

"No no no… I'm happy now, don't say anything just be here with me, leave your work behind along with your worries." Kanak suggested.

"Okay, madam." Samrat agreed with a smile.

Seeing Samrat's pleasant smile, Kanak placed her palm on Samrat's fingers and slowly took his hand making his finger intertwin with hers. Her delicate malleable fingers bring a sense of softness to Samrat's hand, he understood what this sign meant but refused to acknowledge it to tease her knowing she would easily be nettled. And so it happened as expected, after seeing Samrat refusing to understand what she wanted, Kanak immediately tried to take her hand behind, however, Samrat held her fingers and started laughing, finding the irritated expression he was enjoying his wife's rudeness and desire to annoy her more to enjoy this side of her as well.

"You are annoying me now," Kanak said in a bit exasperated tone.

"I love this side of yours" Samrat laughed.

"Of course you do," she replied annoyingly taking her hand behind.

"Come on, I didn't mean to make you angry. I only did it in jest. Also, we can't do what you want in public." Samrat joked.

"What do I want?" she asked.

"You are being amorous. I know but that is so not good to carry out in public plus I am a police officer just imagine what would happen if they caught us getting cozy." Samrat replied

"Don't put your thoughts in my mind. I am not at all thinking about any of those things." Kanak answered.

"That is good, you are a smart baby." Samrat smiled foolishly.

Kanak nodded and again lifted her hand to hold Samrat's hand and this time she held them tightly.

As their conversation continued, Samrat suggested ordering some food. Kanak agreed, and he called over a waiter to request dishes that were both tasty and affordable. Upon perusing the menu, Samrat was taken aback by the steep prices but noted that the restaurant's ambiance had remained unchanged. He shared this observation with Kanak after the waiter departed. Maybe it is because they went out after so long. Though Samrat occasionally ate out, he had never before splurged on a fancy restaurant meal that might exceed his budget. Every so often, he used to get settled for snacks when out late.

As their food was served, both Kanak and Samrat eagerly prepared to indulge in the delectable-looking dishes before them. Upon taking their first bites, they both felt immensely satisfied with their choices.

As they savored their meal, Kanak and Samrat chatted amiably until Samrat abruptly mentioned the name 'Ahilya' The contented moment between them was snapped in an instant, as Kanak heard the name slip from his lips. Initially, She wanted to pretend that she did not hear anything and contemplated feigning ignorance, but Samrat's sudden change of expression and his searching gaze for someone – Ahilya, specifically – captured her attention and eventually she broke her silence on it.

"What?" Kanak asked.

"I think I saw Ahilya here," Samrat answered.

"I guess she's with someone." He continued.

Kanak suggested that they let Ahilya enjoy her dinner without disturbance, hoping that Samrat would agree with her. However, his questioning eyes made it clear that he wanted to know who Ahilya was with. She realized that any further insistence on her part would only lead to a dispute or worse and that Samrat would ultimately do what he pleased.

"I think I should go and check," Samrat said.

"You'll only end up disturbing her," Kanak replied.

"Just a quick greeting won't harm anyone, don't you think?" he countered.

Though Kanak nodded in agreement, Samrat failed to notice and promptly stood up.

"I'll be back in a minute, babe," he said before leaving to look for Ahilya.

Kanak remained numb in her seat, unwilling to turn and confirm whether Ahilya was truly present. She simply wished for everything to transpire quickly, with her name and presence excluded from the situation.

Her eyes remained fixed on the plate of food that she had been enjoying just a few minutes earlier, but she refused to take another bite now. She was fervently hoping that whatever Samrat had witnessed was merely a figment of his imagination and not true. However, her hopes were dashed when she saw Samrat standing beside her with Ahilya and her son Madhav.

Though she sensed their presence next to her, her will was to refuse to look at them, she was jittering but she had to refuse her fear and manage an exchange of smiles because if she didn't it would put her in suspicion and she didn't want her husband to raise any conjecture. And so she slowly lifted her face and moved in the direction where Ahilya was standing, managing a smile on her lips she stood from her place and raised her hand to greet.

"Hello, I'm Kanak, Samrat's wife." She said.

Ahilya didn't reply to her greeting instead Madhav briefed Kanak about Ahilya's condition.

"Oh, I'm sorry, Samrat did tell me about this but I forgot." She apologized.

"It's okay" Madhav replied.

Ahilya was standing next to Madhav, observing Kanak with her uncanny eyes. Meanwhile, Kanak was trying her best enough to avoid any contact with her.

"So, how's now?" Kanak asked.

"She's fine, doing good," Madhav answered.

Kanak smiled and looked at her husband with an expression to leave the place. The kind of look on her face made him understand that his wife was not comfortable being with people on their very special day. However, Samrat did not want to leave the conversation this instant so he assured her to wait for a minute and so and after that, they would exit.

Samrat arranged more chairs for them to join but Madhav politely refused to share his time with them. He explained how he wanted to have dinner with her mother somewhere by themselves so he was looking for a corner in the meantime Samrat saw them and asked them to join so refusing so immediately might make him appear rude hence he cared to at least be introduced to Kanak.

"Oh no, Madhav I totally agree with your opinion. You are with your family, I know how much you care about her, please don't mind Samrat's behavior he is just too involved in his work." Kanak said.

At first, Madhav appreciated her kindness however there was something odd in her kindness, her voice felt familiar to him when he met Kanak for the first time, he could sense the closeness through her words, they sounded different as if she knew something about them more than Samrat, more than anyone of them.

"Samrat, it's okay. We can go home I guess." She continued.

And all four exchanged a goodbye. Samrat and Kanak went out of the place while Ahilya and Madhav found a corner to sit peacefully. The silence of Ahilya was killing Kanak from inside leaving traces of suspicion whether she remembered her or not.

As Madhav took the seat and ordered his and his mother's meal a sense of uncertainty struck him that brought a question to his mind even though he believed that it might be his false assumption still he decided to ask Ahilya about Kanak.

"Why do I feel like she is someone I have met before or her voice is kind of familiar to me," Madhav asked.

"Do you know her?" he continued to ask.

Ahilya did not reply to him, her mind was absent from the time she met Kanak and it brought a sense of familiarity with Kanak's dithering smile, it was the smile that she had seen before but couldn't remember enough to mention where.

"Maa? What are you thinking?"

And after a while, she finally broke her silence.

"Why are we here? Are we dining here?"

"Yes." Madhav sighed.

The waiter came with the order and they dug into their food enjoying every bite of it.

As they continued to eat with the silence surrounding their table, Madhav wanted to break the quietness so he asked the same question again in the hope of getting an answer that could give recompense however, Ahilya had already forgotten what had happened a while ago.

"You didn't bring your book to write down about today,"

"I thought I didn't need it."

"You should carry it everywhere maa, it is important for you."

"I will remember from next time."

Madhav laughed loudly at her sentence and replied with a smile

"You… Okay just remember it from next time."

The ambiguity in his questions where caving him and leading to another thought that he wanted to try on. The voice of Kanak was resounding in his mind and he couldn't afford to overlook it. The moment he met her, he was distracted because for him she sounded like someone, someone whom he had heard before someone who had been around her mother when he was not, someone who he had only heard on the phone but never got the chance to see, someone who was there for her mother when he wasn't.

A flood of questions made his ignorance drown and forced him to take action toward the answer that we wanted to know. He looked at her mother, with a look that could tell how much he wanted his mother to help him in his journey of seeking the answers. The eyes were seeking an answer from his mother that even a hint could lead him to a path otherwise he is walking on a path with vague directions that is leading him to nowhere.

"I wish you could help me, Mom, I wish you could tell me what happened to you, what made you like this or I wish this all could have never happened at all."

"What are you talking about?"

"I am saying that I wanted a peaceful life from the beginning but it never actually happened, does it? I met you and Baba and I thought now I could live happily but look what it turned out to be just a short-term happiness. It was like a weekend that ended before it could start."

"What happened? You are acting strange."

"I am just… Nothing maa, can we order any dessert? Would you like to eat some?"

"Tell me what is bothering you"

"Even if I tell you it will be of no means because… because you won't remember it anyway so let's just pretend that everything is fine."

"Did I do something that is causing you problems? I don't know what I had done or what wrong my deeds were that is causing my child to suffer for me or because of me. I can only ask for your forgiveness."

"Please don't be like this maa you have done nothing wrong."

"I don't know maybe I have done something that is killing you from inside and the sad part is I can't help it. I only remember your presence when you are around, I can only remember your face when I see it."

"It's okay, let's eat something sweet."

"I'm sorry…"

"Madhav"

"Yes, Madhav. I'm sorry Madhav."

"Now, enough with this emotional drama, let me order some dessert to make our evening sweet."

Ahilya smiled and held Madhav's hand like a mother caressing his child. She kissed his palm and assured him that things would be alright.

For a minute, Madhav felt like it was the world to him however it was soon going to be forgotten by her, her caresses, and her apology soon will be forgotten by her but for him, it was forever.

CHAPTER 11
THE CLUE

In the morning when Samrat was getting ready for his work, and Kanak was in the kitchen packing his lunch he could see the despairing face of his wife assuming that she might demand more of his time to be with her. He does want to be around her for a long to pamper her more to listen to her talk and to keep her close to him but his work couldn't allow him to and more importantly his chase for solving the mystery of Ahilya. Because for him this case was no less important and for him, it was a chance. Knowing that his absence would morose his wife and would injure her emotions, he broke his silence by mentioning something that could at least terminate the silence between them.

"I guess I was looking dull yesterday, don't you think?"

Kanak didn't answer his question and silently continued to pack his lunch.

"You looked very sweet."

Kanak packed the lunch and kept it on the table sliding it a little towards the Samrat.

"Babe, I'm sorry but I have to leave and I promise I will take you somewhere nice."

"And yet again you will bring your work there." She finally broke her silence.

"What do you mean?"

"Samrat, you could have just ignored them, I wanted to spend more time there but you brought 'em to our place, why?"

"I thought it would be okay"

"It's not, it's not okay at all. You were supposed to focus on me yet again you chose to ignore me."

"No... no... it's not like that."

"Let me know if you are coming home at night so I can prepare for your dinner as well."

And she left the kitchen and walked towards her bedroom but before she could close the door she turned back and stared at Samrat with her teary eyes.

"I wanted it to be our night you know... our!"

Closing the door behind her she disappeared from Samrat's sight leaving him alone in the room where he stood with a dejected face accepting his blunder. He took the packed lunch and waited for a minute in anticipation of Kanak opening the door and coming back to him to at least say to him bye however it did not happen and he left the home.

Hearing the door closing behind Samrat, she came out of the room apprehensively as if she was waiting for him to leave. Her face has been changed from the moment before she was with Samrat and now she seemed to be more worried over something. The look on her face was different, it wasn't something that had happened because of Samrat it was something that she had suffered already, and yet again the same ache ran through her veins leading to the pain that only she could endure. The thoughts that she wanted to let slip away again knocked and along with it welcomed the anxiety inside her. Her blood was rushing inside her veins and she could hear her heartbeats gradually increasing and she was able to hear them loud. She was straying in the room thinking something that could help her to overcome her situation. Scratching every possibility on how to escape from the blunder that has come back in her life, she finally agreed with one of her options.

She considered this idea would help her to finally find peace from Ahilya and that she could easily turn the wheel around because she knew there had been no clue that could lead anything to her so she decided to execute her step. The step that she believed would finally settle everything that she had been pursuing for long enough and she believed that this would be the end of it, the end of her endurance, and the suffering that was gifted by Ahilya to her.

Before she could plot she wanted to discover what had happened already regarding the case, she wanted to learn every step of Samrat's investigation however asking him directly would create suspicion between them and she refused to take any risk in her plan. But what else could she do to know what has been happening? Samrat would be of no help for her she thought. And she couldn't afford to hire a detective who would help her the same. Whatever she had to do it was all on her own. Though she was content with her idea of misleading everyone yet the process would seem to be quite strenuous and demanding. But she couldn't step back from her idea because if she did it would be the end of her life, her happiness, and her attempt to lead a peaceful life with her husband.

But before any inception, it was required to get the information regarding the investigation she thought that asking Samrat would be suspicious, and so she had to make her way to find out things. She sat on the chair in the kitchen and began to play around with her finger making a circle on the table thinking hard enough to get any idea. After fathom she decided to go to the place, the place where she had experienced the worst of her life, the place that had changed her whole world, the place that filled her life with haunting thoughts. However, visiting the place required to be kept hidden from Samrat and Madhav, she thought. And it was also necessary to not let anyone raise an inch of doubt in her as she had already understood how her husband had already made himself aware of that place. But will that be any help, visiting the place before knowing what had been happening? She thought. Even though she goes there what are the chances that she would be able to fetch out any clue? She thought again. Or maybe it would be better to not visit but to somehow try to find out about the progress in the case. And this could only happen with the help of Samrat because he knew the things as he was involved diligently in it.

"I can ask Samrat but…" she sounded uncertain.

"Asking him can raise suspicion and I can't afford it right now… I can't lose after this long." She continued.

Asking her husband straightaway about Ahilya can gradually build a wall of doubts and it might end against Kanak. Hence she chose an act of fooling her husband that could lead him to cough out all the happenings about the Ahilya.

"Think… think… think something damn it, you can just sit around," she thought.

Biting her nails she continued to think hard about an act to carry in front of Samrat. Considering their current situation, she couldn't instantly turn into a sweet wife and refuse all the fuss that had happened a day prior, that's not who Kanak is, and being like that will definitely make her a skeptical person in front of him. She can't fool her husband with that. While her sweetness might make her skeptical, it is her anger that consistently prompts him to express his thoughts. She knew it better and thus she was certain enough to carry an act of furiousness that would make Samrat tell her everything about Ahilya and his approach towards the truth.

But before she could jump to it, she decided to prepare her mind enough to sustain herself in the act because she had the idea about how her husband could shift from being gentle to indignant in seconds, and she was familiar enough with how she could be easily let her anger get heavy on her hence she was taking her time to get prepared mentally to handle things in her favor.

After settling on her idea she went inside the kitchen looking for her phone. She wanted to call Samrat to ask him whether he would be coming home or not but then she remembered saying that she had already made herself clear that she least cared about him being in the house by saying that he should let her know his availability. And since she had already made this situation it would be wrong if she took the risk of asking him for dinner.

She stopped herself from doing so and believed that it would be better to wait for him to come by himself. After that, she wanted to shift her mind from all the thoughts that were hindering her idea and those thoughts were making her lose her hold on her plan so she decided to slide it out by making herself a lunch meal. She stepped inside the kitchen room opened the refrigerator and took out a capsicum, and a tomato. Placing them on the table she went to take the knife from the knife holder and as her palm touched the handle of the knife a flashback hit her so hard that she was agitated. It was from the day when she was fighting for her life, one of the worst days that she was trying to forget. But now that day is again haunting her. The time she thought that everything would be gone, it came back to her… and now she couldn't escape from it.

She took a step back and managed to fix herself, she was aware enough of how to handle herself considering everything she had been through she was able to manage herself with such situations. Depriving herself she sat on the chair for a minute staring at the knife when she finally decided to take the knife in her hand. She stood up and took the knife from the knife holder and started cutting the vegetables. She involved herself in making herself the lunch so that no thoughts could make her weak.

Being busy preparing her lunch for a while has disconnected her from all the thoughts that have been chasing her since she met Ahilya. After finishing, she poured some water into a glass and kept it on the table, taking a plate she kept a bowl on it and kept them on the table next to the glass of water. Then she took the cauldron in which she cooked vegetable gravy and placed it near the glass of water. The last thing she took was the airtight pot in which she cooked rice for herself. Considering herself the only one who is going to eat the lunch she cooked a minimum amount of meal so that nothing should be kept for leftovers. She un-lid the airtight pot took a ladle of rice and served herself, then she took the same ladle and took a ladle full of vegetable gravy and added it to the rice. She mixed it with her fingers and before she took a bite her cell phone started ringing. She stood up and went inside the bedroom to receive the call. When she took her phone, the call was hung up, it was Samrat's call. She thought of calling him back and so she dialed the number but then the phone rang again and it was Samrat.

"Hey," Samrat said.

"Yes," she replied.

"Are you still angry with me?" he asked.

"Do you want something?" she said in a cold voice.

"I'll be home at night. I want to have…"

"I will make dinner for you, anything else?" she said without letting him finish his sentence.

"Okay, no nothing else."

"Shall I hang up now?"

"Yeah bye."

She hung up the phone without saying anything after Samrat's 'bye' and went to the dining table to eat her meal.

She thought that now Samrat would be home by night then it would be her chance to make him uncover all the things that he had discovered while investigating Ahilya's case. She was prepared to make her move. She was waiting for the night to arrive.

When Samrat pressed the doorbell the sound of it made Kanak's heart instantly start pounding so loud that she could hear her heartbeats. Though she had heard the doorbell yet she refused to open the door at first. When Samrat pressed the bell again, it was then she moved towards the door keeping herself calm, letting herself into the character.

She opened the door and immediately turned back without seeing Samrat's face. Samrat stepped inside the apartment and stood at the doorway for a few seconds to see whether his wife would turn back to see him but nothing much happened and he went to his bedroom without a word.

After getting freshened up, he went to the kitchen where he saw a bowl filled with Dal, two chappatis, sliced tomato, and onion along with gravy that was already served on a plate and Kanak was having her dinner sitting opposite the chair where he was supposed to sit. Seeing his wife being distant from him was something that made him insecure, he couldn't agree to this silence and the distance between them.

"You already started?" Samrat asked taking the chair behind to sit.

"Yes," she replied refusing to look at him.

"How long will you stay like this?" he asked.

"I don't know" she continued to eat.

"Babe, I am sorry."

"You are always sorry."

"Can we just forget about that for once? Please Kanak"

"Sure, this is what I do always… you tell me to forget and I do as you say."

"I am sorry."

"Why is she getting all the importance Samrat? Why?"

She finally threw her initial attempt.

"She's not important."

"Yeah, she is… Of course, she is, you ruined our night for her, you invited her to have dinner with us in the middle of our date."

"It was…"

"What?"

"I thought there might be something I mean we could have talked about their history, more about how she was, something more about their life."

Hearing Samrat's reply brought a sudden uncertainty inside Kanak however, she disallowed her emotions to take control. She managed to be in a state of furious instead of edgy.

"Why did you want to know their history… their life?"

"It was nothing Kanak, it was nothing. I JUST SAW THEM! I felt like I should invite them."

"But why? It was supposed to be us, JUST US!"

She banged her fist on the table.

"Kanak!"

"No! Do you have any idea how much I crave for us to be together? No. You have always, always kept others above me, every FUCKING time. Why do you involve work everywhere? Why?"

"Can you please relax? Please."

"I have lost my patience. I have lost my patience Samrat. I know why you asked them to join us, yes, you were looking for a lead, a clue that would elevate your so-called investigation. Correct me if I am wrong. Being with you made me realize that I am the only one who enjoys being around you, it's not vice-versa, is it? You are always busy, every fucking day! You don't come home at night and I used to complain about it but then I got used to it, and you never found it strange. I cry myself to sleep Samrat, I stay awake at night for you. I don't say my worries that does not mean I am okay with this. Just because I carry it well it does not mean it ain't heavy, Samrat."

She dug her face into her hands.

"Kanak, I am sorry."

"Oh yes, you are sorry. So you felt like you should ask them to join. Why? So that you could look for a clue, yes. You were just looking for a clue... A clue? Everywhere? Anytime? So tell me did you find any?"

She threw her second attempt.

"Nothing."

"How come nothing? You have been following her case, you must have got something."

"I said nothing."

"Come on, it's not nothing I know, what did you find?"

"Kanak stop it."

"I won't. Tell me how much you found about her. Is it enough to promote you?"

"Enough now!"

"Tell me! Is it enough to promote you?"

"No, it's not... NO, okay? NO. Nothing had happened, no clue other than a girl who was living with Ahilya. Her son is looking for her, I have already told you all this. Yes, I involve work everywhere because I want to give you a good life."

"A good life where you are not around? Do you think I will enjoy it?"

"It will be good for us babe."

For a minute there were no words that could be listened to or heard. Kanak quietly ate her supper and once she was done she slightly moved her plate and broke the silence.

"I think I want to go home to my parents."

"Kanak?"

"Please, don't contact me there or don't tell them about us. I need to be away for some days."

"Fine. If that's what you want."

"I'll let you know when I'll be coming here, you don't have to be worried. I mean you usually don't so."

"Fine."

She took the plate and kept it in the sink, washed her hands under the tap water, and left the place. When she left the room, Samrat frustratingly pushed the table, making his dal spill. The frustration inside him made him angrier and seeing the distance growing between them was something he felt painful though this distance has been faced enough times before however this time it was longing for something else, something unwillingly distorting making their relationship weak and suffering.

CHAPTER 12
THE CHOICE

The following morning, Samrat awoke in a drowsy state, rubbing his eyes gently. He noticed Kanak, in the process of packing her clothes into a bag. He felt the urge to apologize once again, but deep down, he knew that neither an apology nor a hug would mend the uncertainty that plagued their relationship. The idea of his wife's quibbling and distancing herself from him was unsettling for Samrat. Although he desired to voice his objections, he refrained, aware that it would only complicate matters further. In Samrat's eyes, Kanak's decision to leave the house was his own fault, and he sadly acknowledged that there was nothing he could do but watch her leave.

When Kanak finished packing her clothes, she shifted her gaze toward Samrat. Her face displayed a frown, her grip tightened on the bag's handle, and she finally broke the uncomfortable silence between them.

"I'm going to my parent's house," she stated.

Samrat nodded in acknowledgment, avoiding direct eye contact he replied "Yes,"

With the bag's handle in her grasp, Kanak pulled it off the bed and began walking towards the door. As she opened the door, the sound caught Samrat's attention, causing him to look in Kanak's direction. He watched her leave.

The absence of his wife made the house feel desolate, Samrat contemplated, and he had no desire to engage in any activities to escape from this void. Enduring the pain seemed like the only path toward accepting it. Once his wife had departed, he rose from the bed, leaving the sheets untouched. Leaving the lights and fan running, he exited his bedroom and proceeded to freshen up. Every action felt contrary to his own will, yet he had to prepare for his job. After getting ready, he entered the kitchen and discovered that breakfast had already been laid out for him. There was a plate with brown bread alongside a jar of mango jam, accompanied by a spoon. Placed beneath the plate was a small note that mentioned, 'Serve tea by yourself. Warm it first.' Samrat read the note, placed it on the table, and pulled out a chair to take a seat. He opened the jar of jam, scooped out a spoonful, and spread it onto the bread. While doing so, he noticed that something was written on the reverse side of the small note. Curiously, he picked up the note and turned it over, only to find something that deepened his melancholy. The note contained the message, 'I will come when I want to.'

Having finished his breakfast, he began searching for his phone in his pockets, but it eluded his grasp. Consequently, he headed back to his bedroom and scoured the bed until he located it near the pillow. Retrieving his phone, he dialed a familiar number: Durgesh's.

"Durgesh, everything alright at the station?" he inquired.

"Yes, sir. Just a few minor cases that don't require your attention," Durgesh responded.

"Alright."

"Sir, have you discovered anything regarding the case of the old woman?"

"I believe I won't be coming to the station today. Let me know if there are any updates. Please manage things for a while," he requested.

"Of course, sir. Are you alright?" Durgesh inquired.

"Yes, I'm fine."

Ending the call, he casually tossed the phone onto the bed, leaving the bedroom as it was. Stepping into the living room, he noticed the TV remote resting on the table in front of the couch. He picked it up and switched on the television, settling himself comfortably on the couch. As he flicked through the channels, he failed to find anything that captured his interest. His mind was entangled in a web of various thoughts, preventing him from finding solace in a single moment.

The stillness within the house, the void left by Kanak's voice and her physical presence, was something Samrat yearned to experience. When she was present, he never grew weary of her company and constantly sought solace in it. Now that she had departed, he found himself longing for her presence, her gentle touch, her spontaneous conversations, and the distinct phrase 'You know...' that she used before sharing any incidents or stories with him.

After some time, he reached over and turned off the television. Resting his head on the couch, he struggled to find inner tranquility. Slowly, he closed his eyes and drifted into sleep.

In his slumber, he found himself in an outdoor setting, bathed in the afternoon sunlight. A man dressed in a white shirt stood before a vessel, stirring its contents with a ladle. His speech was slanted, and his voice distorted, yet a few words managed to be audible. He spoke about a girl.

"She used to live... I know... I only showed her the place," the man uttered.

Although there appeared to be no one else present, he seemed to be conversing with an unseen entity.

"Yes, there was a girl... no, two girls," he continued.

"What? What did you say?" a distorted male voice echoed.

Then, a clear female voice resonated—Kanak's voice.

"You are still searching for them? Am I nothing to you?" she questioned.

"Kanak," the man acknowledged.

Meanwhile, Samrat slumbered, his forehead damp with sweat, muttering in his sleep. The voice of the man in the white shirt gradually grew louder, echoing through his dream. The man persistently repeated, 'Yes, there was a girl... no, two girls,' while Kanak's voice persistently asked in a heightened pitch, 'You are still searching for them?' Sweat gradually drenched Samrat's face, a manifestation of fear or uncertainty that occurred unbeknownst to him. He suddenly awoke, gasping for breath, his face flushed, and his t-shirt collar moist with perspiration. He wiped his forehead with his hand and made his way to the kitchen for a glass of water.

As he sipped the water, his mind was consumed by thoughts of the dream he had just experienced.

"What was that? Damn! What was that man trying to tell me... He seemed familiar, but who was he?" he pondered.

He set the glass aside and took a seat, determined to delve into his memory and extract any possible information from the dream.

"He was stirring... what? Who was he? The tea stall owner? Why did he infiltrate my dream, and why did he mention two girls again? I already know he mentioned it to me, so why did I dream about it? What did I miss? Am I losing my grip... is there some kind of obstacle? Fuck, I needed a break!

And why Kanak's voice... why did I hear her voice? What the hell was she... What's amiss here?"

"I needed a break!" he cried.

He covered his face with his hands and sat in contemplation for a while. After some time, he lifted his face and gently rubbed his temples.

"I don't think a break would make any difference. I know Kanak is upset, but this case won't let me find peace. I have to unravel the mystery behind Ahilya's scream."

As he reclined on the couch, he rested his head and delved into deep contemplation, attempting to connect the dots recorded in his compact notebook. Now that he possessed a better understanding of Madhav's history and his relationship with Ahilya, he felt confident enough to shift his focus away from his own narrative and explore other angles that could establish connections. With his gaze fixed upon the rotating ceiling fan, he began amalgamating all the observations he had made thus far in the case.

"She keeps screaming about the dead body that she has seen, but there isn't any that means there might have happened to be a dead body. This is the first thing that I need to know. And so she used to live in that house where she claims to have seen a dead body it means there's something wrong in that place. As per Madhav and that tea stall owner there were two girls living with her in that house. I need to find out who were they. And the house was burnt and looks like it was left as it is but what about the things in the house and who was there when the house was burnt, what about those two girls? Didn't they see anything? What about that house? I should have a closer look at it, there must be information about it when the incident happened. I should ask for the report from the department."

Prompted to locate his phone, he glanced around but failed to spot it, leading him to utter spontaneously, "Kanak, have you seen my phone?" A pause followed by a question that he knew had no answer at the moment, he ran his fingers gently through his hair, left the couch, and ventured into the bedroom to search for his phone, which he found resting on the bed. Switching on the screen, he discovered his and Kanak's image as the wallpaper, evoking a serene smile on his face, intermingled with unexpected sorrows. Setting aside his emotions, he tossed the screen, unlocked his phone, and proceeded to dial Durgesh's number.

"Hello, Durgesh, is everything good?"

"Yes, sir, everything is good so far."

"Actually, I need some information regarding a case stored in our database. I need your help."

"Yes, sir, please say."

"I want you to search for a case involving a house that was burnt in flames approximately 8 or 9 years ago. The address is Nirlon Park, Goregaon."

"Nirlon Park?"

"Yes, please do what I asked for. I need to determine if any incident took place there. Please send me the report via WhatsApp if you find anything."

"Alright, sir."

CHAPTER 13
THE ACCEPTANCE

"Have you discovered anything, any information about the girl? Have you reached out to your sources? Can you actually accomplish something? This situation is going nowhere!" Madhav exclaimed in frustration over the phone.

"Find her, man! Find her!" he exclaimed once more before abruptly ending the call. He stowed the phone in his pants pocket and vented his anger by forcefully punching the table before him. The impact caused the glass of water, which he had placed there a few minutes earlier upon returning from his mother's apartment, to topple over, spilling its contents onto the floor. This aggravated him further, as his mother had once again claimed to have seen a bloodied man lying on the floor, marking the second instance that day.

Despite being aware that repeating the same question to everyone he knew, even remotely connected to his mother, would not yield different answers, he persisted in his inquiries. Disregarding the fallen glass and the water that now adorned the floor, he proceeded to his bedroom and retrieved his wallet. Slipping it into his back pocket, he commenced a search for his keys.

"Where did I put them?" he muttered to himself. In a hurry, he entered the kitchen and began scouring for the keys. He checked the refrigerator, where he usually stored his assortment of fancy cups, and inspected the wall where he habitually hung his keys. Exiting the kitchen, he patted his pockets to ensure the keys were not already in his possession. His gaze shifted to the vicinity of the television, where he spotted the keys hanging from the door's lock. It dawned on him that he had left them there upon returning to his apartment after consoling his mother. Retrieving the keys, he tucked them away in his back pocket, closed the door, and left the premises.

The sole thought occupying his mind as he left the house was the girl. She represented the only lead he had in his mother's case, and he was eager to acquire any information about her. Despite realizing that asking the tea stall owner the same question again would likely yield no new answers, he still desired to make another attempt. He believed that even receiving the same response could provide a different perspective that might lead him to a new breakthrough.

As he approached the tea stall, he noticed the owner closing up shop. Witnessing this, he hurried towards him, calling out, "Hey!" in a rush.

"Oh, sir, hello," the stall owner turned around to greet Madhav.

"Leaving soon?" Madhav asked.

"Yes, yes, I have to take my kid to the hospital," the owner explained.

"Why? What happened? Is everything okay?" Madhav expressed concern.

"Nothing serious, sir, just a fever," the stall owner reassured.

"But what brings you here?" the stall owner asked.

"The same reason as always, you know why I come to you—either regarding the woman or for tea," Madhav replied.

"I'm sorry sir, but I can't help you with either of those today."

"I understand. But please, do you have any additional information? Anything at all? Something new? About those girls? Any details?"

"Sir, I have told you already about the girls. There were two girls and both of them left when that lady was in the hospital."

"I know that you have mentioned this previously."

"What else can you expect? But wait... one thing that makes me wonder is that..."

"What?"

"Ahilya madam was already in the hospital, and both of the girls had left her. So how did the apartment catch fire?"

"What do you mean?"

"The fire occurred after Ahilya madam was admitted to the hospital. If no one was present, how did the house catch fire?"

The tea stall owner gathered his belongings and requested that Madhav not prolong their conversation.

"I have to go, sir. I don't know much about it."

"Yes, yes, please take good care of your son, and if you need anything, don't hesitate to let me know."

Unaware of how his former apartment had succumbed to the flames, Madhav used to believe that everything happened while his mother, Ahilya, resided there. However, the tea stall owner's words introduced a new piece of information to him. This revelation further intensified his doubts about the girls and strengthened his determination to locate them.

With this newfound information, he embarked towards his apartment, contemplating who could have ignited the fire. Was it intentional? And if so, why? The fire wasn't meant to harm his mother, so what was the motive behind it? Numerous questions swirled in his mind, yearning for answers that Madhav couldn't find at that moment.

Instead of heading to his own apartment upon arrival, he approached Ahilya's door and knocked, patiently awaiting her response. The first knock went unanswered, prompting him to try a second time. Finally, she opened the door, and Madhav greeted her with a smile, prompting her to welcome him inside.

"What brings you here?" she asked, proceeding to the kitchen to fetch a glass of water for him.

"Forget again? You invited me for dinner," he reminded her.

"I did?" she questioned while handing him the water.

"Of course, you did. Why else would I be here?" he replied playfully.

"I don't remember."

"Obviously, you don't remember," he teased.

"I don't remember anything. I know."

"It's okay, maa. I'm just messing with you. You didn't invite me for dinner; it was my idea to eat with you."

"Maa?" she questioned, surprised.

"I can call you maa, can't I?"

"Okay, I'm your maa."

"You were always my maa," he murmured softly.

"Can I help you with anything? No, wait, I'll prepare dinner for us. You go and rest," he offered kindly.

"Why should I rest? I can cook. Let me prepare dinner, and you can wait," she insisted, heading into the kitchen.

"Okay, but I won't wait outside. I want to watch you cook. I used to enjoy seeing you prepare meals. You used to sing while cooking, and Papa used to join in," he reminisced.

"Did I really do that? But how did you see me cooking? Did we live together before?" she asked, puzzled.

"Maa, you ask so many questions now. Come on, focus on cooking. What are you making? Let me guess... It seems like rice and vegetable gravy with a sunny-side-up omelet. I love this combination," he guessed.

She smiled.

"Is it ready already?" he asked.

"Yes, only the omelet is remaining," she replied.

"Let me handle that while you take the food to the table," he said.

She picked up the plates and the water jug, placing them on the dining table adjacent to the kitchen. Meanwhile, Madhav finished one omelet and began preparing the next. Ahilya poured the vegetable gravy into a large bowl and placed it on the table, followed by the cooked rice. Before settling down, she started serving the meal onto each plate and asked Madhav if he was done with the omelets.

"Come soon, the food is getting cold."

Madhav approached the table with a plate of omelets and set it in the center.

"I'm done," he announced.

Both of them began to enjoy their meal in silence. Ahilya seemed to relish her supper, while Madhav, on the other hand, was eager to ask her a few questions, even though he anticipated the same response. Still, his curiosity compelled him to inquire.

"Did you see that man covered in blood again?" he finally broke the silence.

"Why do you ask? I don't know anything about a man," she responded.

He stood up and walked over to the refrigerator, where he discovered a sticky note attached to it. The note read, 'I saw the man again on June 24th, 2023.'

"You wrote this already," he remarked.

"I wish I could answer your questions, but I can't," she replied.

"It's alright, maa," he said, turning back to his dinner. However, his attention was suddenly drawn to another sticky note. He went to examine it once again, and it read, 'A girl was sitting next to a man covered in blood on June 18th, 2023.' He removed the note from the refrigerator and showed it to Ahilya.

"You wrote this," he stated.

"Maybe," she replied, taking another bite of her food.

"This is something new, maa. We've found a new lead," he exclaimed.

"What do you mean?" she asked.

"It's nothing," he responded, returning to his chair and placing the sticky note beside him.

"Let's continue with our dinner," he suggested.

"Did I invite you for dinner?" she asked.

"Yes, maa. You forgot again. You invited me for dinner and made those omelets for us," he reminded her.

"Okay," she acknowledged.

"Do you remember my name?" he asked playfully.

At first, she hesitated to answer, but a glimmer of recognition flickered within her. She felt like she knew the answer, although her memory struggled to retrieve his name.

She took a moment and finally replied, "Madhav, you are Madhav."

Upon hearing his name from his mother's lips, a radiant smile spread across his face, as if there was nothing else in the world he could desire more than his mother remembering him and his name.

CHAPTER 14
THE BOOK AND THE POLAROID

A week has passed, and Samrat remained without any word from Kanak. Despite his desire to call her and ask her about her well-being and her return to their home, he found himself lacking the courage to do so. She had explicitly instructed him not to initiate contact, and he understood her behavior well enough to know that she would not answer his call unless she wanted to. Consequently, he concluded that it would be wiser to maintain his distance and patiently await her initiative.

As he contemplated his personal circumstances, Samrat found himself resigned to a state of waiting. He yearned for his wife to return, to accept his apologies, acknowledge his mistakes, and forgive him once again, as she always had. The thoughts of the day Kanak left, leaving both him and their home, consumed him. He became increasingly entangled in the superficiality of their relationship, desperately hoping for improvement with the passage of time. However, this time, the unexpected nature of the situation heightened his sense of unease.

Absorbed in his own thoughts, Samrat failed to register his surroundings as he found himself in the police station, examining the report provided by Constable Durgesh, which he had requested a week prior. The report pertained to a house that had been engulfed in flames approximately 8 to 9 years ago. Although Durgesh stood beside him, eagerly anticipating Samrat's review of the report, he noticed Samrat's distant demeanor and refrained from asking whether this was indeed the report he had sought.

"It seems his mind is preoccupied," Durgesh remarked, then went away from Samrat's side and left the police station altogether.

Lost in his own thoughts, Samrat's attention was abruptly interrupted by the vibrating phone in his hand. It was a message from his mobile service provider, reminding him about his daily internet usage. Unaware of the happenings around him, he composed himself in the chair, ensuring his posture was proper, and glanced at the phone to discover the open report. Drawing the phone closer, he began to meticulously read every detail.

The report provided details regarding an apartment that had been destroyed by fire approximately 8-9 years ago. Unfortunately, there were no witnesses present in or around the apartment who could shed light on the incident. The report did not contain any additional information as nobody was able to explain what had occurred. The apartment was completely burned down, and it appears that nothing else was discovered at the scene except for a book and a phone.

Samrat, while reading the report, repeated the phrase "a book and a phone."

He realized that since the area fell under their department's jurisdiction, these items should have been preserved. However, he couldn't comprehend how the fire had gone unnoticed until it engulfed the entire place. He also wondered about the whereabouts mentioned in the report and why no one ever came to retrieve their belongings.

"The area falls under our department and if these two things were found then we must have it saved in the department. But how come no one came to realize about the fire before it took over the place." He thought.

Although the information in the report was jumbled, Samrat was certain that something was amiss in that apartment or that something unfortunate had taken place there. Upon further examination of the report, his suspicions were confirmed. There was definitely something unsettling about that apartment, something ominous, something peculiar, something worse.

"There must have been an event of some kind in that location that needs to be revealed," he pondered.

"I don't understand how the entire place was reduced to ashes, leaving only the book and phone behind. Why does it feel like that place is concealing a secret? I need to investigate the premises, but before that, I must obtain those items that were discovered in the house."

After analyzing everything from the reading he concluded to find the belongings and then visit the place however looking for belongings can be done by someone else what was more important for him was the visit to that burnt apartment. He took his diary out from his table's drawer and began noting the points keeping in mind to achieve them as soon as possible.

First, he wrote about visiting the apartment, second, he noted about the book and the phone that was found in the apartment. After noting the two points he underlined the first one and closed his diary and put it back in the table's drawer. Now that he was aware of one thing about the case, he couldn't resist discovering the clues and taking the investigation in a new way, as he thought of visiting the burnt apartment simultaneously he also realized that he could ask Durgesh to look into those found things. He took his cell phone and dialed his number, the phone was ringing however he didn't receive the call. So, Samrat tried to dial his number again however he stopped himself from calling him as he saw him coming into the police station. Durgesh was approaching Samrat.

"Did you check the report?" Durgesh asked as he came near to Samrat.

"Yes, but that report seems to be... I don't know. You tell me Durgesh how come everything in an apartment is burnt I mean just a book and a phone is left what about everything else?" Samrat asked.

"I think... our police department might have dumped the other things and only kept those two."

"What?"

"I don't know... no one took any interest in that house as far as I know because I am here for the past 5-6 years and none of us or others have ever asked me or anyone around about that place."

"Okay oh yes I think I will take a look at those found things. Can you please do one more thing?"

"Yes sir please ask."

"Can you please help me in looking for those things I mean right now..."

"Of course. Let me just finish one or two things from my side and then I'll join you."

"Thank you very much. You're being such a good friend."

Samrat smiled and patted Durgesh's shoulder.

"Now you are embarrassing me."

Officer Rao sitting on his desk looking into his phone was peeking into the conversations that were happening between Durgesh and Samrat. Though he wanted to come in between them and ask what was going on in-between them but refused to do so as he knew Samrat would refuse to tell him anything and instead he would mock him and make him feel down. But all those things for Rao were not new yet he chose to keep himself away from the conversation and thought to talk privately with Durgesh once Samrat was not around.

Unaware of Rao's eyes on him, Samrat took his phone and keys and went inside a room in the police station where all found things were stored. As soon as he saw him leaving he didn't wait for a second or two and approached Durgesh.

"You two seem to be getting along quite lately" Rao joked.

"Why do you ask sir?" Durgesh smiled.

"Nothing just asking whether there is something you want to tell me or something you should mention."

"No, I don't think there's anything as such important"

"Okay. By the way, did he tell you where he is going?"

"Does he ever tell anyone?"

"Yeah, okay then continue your work."

"Okay, sir."

Durgesh went to his place by disclosing nothing to Rao and keeping his and Samrat's conversation private. For him, Samrat was one of the good officers and not just an officer but an individual as well; he has always appreciated him and helped him in every possible way.

While stepping toward his place he sensed that Rao's eyes were still craving for something, something that would help him to find a reason that he could showcase Samrat's ignorance towards the cases and get involved with something other than that in the presence of seniors. So he decided to not look for the belongings right away but to wait for Rao to complete his shift and leave. He has observed that Rao has started taking an interest in Samrat again and this might once again hinder Samrat's investigation and whatsoever he is into.

Durgesh did his work in a hurry so that he could help Samrat in looking for things. He has always favored him and trusted him as one of the officers on whom he could rely and it was not intuitional. There were times when Samrat had helped him in his work as well while looking around at the work that was considered to be completed by him. Sometimes Samrat used to look after the pending things that Durgesh was supposed to work on, however, he couldn't due to his children and wife. Durgesh was quite bad at managing the balance between his profession and personal life and due to that, he had faced problems in both terms. Hence helping Samrat seemed to be a duty for him and he had always cared for whatever demands Samrat had asked for.

Once done with his side of work, he immediately went on the way where Samrat had asked him. On reaching the store room, he called Samrat's name as soon as he opened the door.

"Sir?"

"Yes, Durgesh come here."

He followed the voice and tried to look for Samrat. Samrat was standing against a shelf with the book that he found among those things. Durgesh while looking for him, found Samrat with a book and started walking towards him.

"Sir, did you find it?" Durgesh asked curiously

"Yeah." Samrat sounded concerned.

"Just a book? Where's the phone?" Durgesh questioned.

"I... I have it with me."

"What happened, sir? You seem a little worried."

"Nothing. I think I should go home nevertheless my shift is over."

He took the things with him and began to walk towards the door, Durgesh couldn't understand this behavior of him and he immediately went to ask him again about what had happened however Samrat was gone from the place. He followed him towards his vehicle quietly with the thought of asking him but refused to say anything as he realized Samrat was a bit off after finding the things and asking him anything would make the situation worse hence he thought of skipping the thought and saw him leaving the police station in commotion.

Samrat is in a state of disturbance and skepticism, opens the door of his car, and throws the book on the next seat. As the book was thrown it made some of the Polaroid photos come out of it. Samrat got into the car and stared at the book and the photos that were half out.

"This is new in this twisted story." He said, staring at the photos.

Taking a Polaroid from the book he looked at the photo, it was a photo of a girl sitting on a couch and smiling. Samrat looked at the image curiously and then slowly turned it back. On the back of it, a four-digit number was written that read '7000'.

"7000?" Samrat said confusedly.

"What does this mean?" he questioned again.

Keeping the Polaroid back at the place he started the car's engine and left the place thinking about the girl in the photo and the number written on the back of it made him forget about the phone which he was carrying along with him.

"Oh, the phone." He said placing his hand inside the left pocket of his pants taking out the phone and keeping it on the book. It was a keypad phone that seemed to be an outdated model.

"I need to get this phone repaired... there might be something in it," he said.

"But will it be working?" He thought.

"I don't think that anyone ever noticed these two things or even cared to get this phone repaired. But what would have been useful? The phone itself looks like... this model is so old. I wonder if anyone will care to repair it. But this seems to be a good sign in the case and I have to take the opportunity."

And with all the conversations he had with himself while driving back home, he finally realized that he had reached his home. He parked the car and before he kept the photo back inside the book he took the book along with the phone and stepped out of the car.

While opening the door of his house, he took a big sigh and unlocked the door thinking if only he could see Kanak's face after the long day, if only he could eat the dinner made by her hand, and if only he could sleep next to her watching her beautiful face while she's sleeping. All these thoughts brought a certain sadness onto his face and as he stepped inside the house, the emptiness surrounded him.

Shutting the door behind he went directly into the kitchen, he kept the book and the phone on the table and began to look for the leftovers that he could at least taste and take a sleep. He removed the lid of a small metal pot and found some remaining dal in it. Keeping the metal pot on the gas he lit the stove and began to look for a glass. As his eyes gave a glance over the kitchen he could see that there were no clean utensils left in the house on which he could pour the dal. All were in the sink left to be washed. Finding no utensils he did not bother to wash any of them, and turned the stove off and went into his bedroom taking the book and the phone.

The bedroom appeared to be a messed up room that had not been cleaned in the past few days. The pillows were improperly lying on each side of the bed, the bed sheet was unfolded and half of the bed was covered from untidy clothes. The messiness of the room explained how recklessly Samrat had been living his days without Kanak. Though he had thoughts of going against Kanak's promise to call her he still couldn't collect all the guts to dial her number and make her come back to him.

He carefully stored the book within the rearmost drawer of the cupboard, right above the very same book he had brought back with him from Ahilya's abode. Concurrently, he placed his phone within the confines of his trouser pocket. After securely shutting the cupboard, he proceeded to retire for the night.

CHAPTER 15
THE PLANS SHE MADE

In the blistering heat, Kanak stood with a handbag draped over her left shoulder, wearing white jeans and a black satin top, standing across K.M College, her face partly covered by a scarf that revealed only her eyes. The frequency with which she checked her phone suggested her intense eagerness to meet someone. Although her constant phone-checking occasionally made her agitated, she was careful not to appear dubious to people where she was standing. She patiently awaited someone's arrival, while a clothing shop situated behind her seemed to have an owner growing increasingly uneasy about her presence.

With a furrowed brow, the shop owner called a worker from inside and irritably questioned why a woman – Kanak, was standing in front of their store. The worker offered the possibility that she might be waiting for someone. However, the owner couldn't fathom why she didn't choose another spot to wait.

"Can't she go somewhere else if she's waiting for someone?" he grumbled.

"I don't believe she's causing any trouble for us," the worker responded.

"Don't try to outsmart me," retorted the owner.

"I'm not trying to," the worker insisted.

"She's driving away our customers," the owner claimed.

"We haven't had any customers since morning, and she's been here for just fifteen minutes," reasoned the worker.

"Don't try to school me on running my business," the owner snapped.

"But..." the worker tried to interject.

"Just go and ask her to move away from the entrance," the owner ordered, exasperated.

"Fine," sighed the worker, complying reluctantly.

The shop worker emerged from the store, politely requesting that Kanak leave the area since the owner was getting agitated with someone standing in front of the shop.

"I'm hardly blocking anything. I highly doubt my presence is affecting your customer traffic," Kanak replied.

"I understand, ma'am, but my boss can be difficult," the worker explained.

"To be honest, that doesn't make much sense. I've been here for fifteen minutes, and no one has passed by or shown any interest in the shop. How could I be causing an obstruction?" Kanak questioned.

"I know and I even told him the same thing, but I still have to ask you to leave," the worker said.

The shop owner was cocking an ear to the conversation between Kanak and the worker and finally decided to step outside.

"What's happening?" he asked, sounding indignant.

"Nothing, sir," the worker replied politely.

"I request that you move away from this spot and stand somewhere else madam," the owner said to Kanak.

"I will, but I'm waiting for someone, and I don't believe I'm causing any trouble for you guys, really I haven't seen anyone walking into your shop." Kanak retorted.

"That is not your business, please move away from our shop and find another spot. You're blocking the entrance," the owner insisted.

"You guys..." Kanak let out a sarcastic laugh, taking a few steps to stand beneath a nearby tree.

"Now are you satisfied?" she called out.

The owner remained silent and went back inside the shop, followed by the worker.

"Isn't it unbelievable how rude people are these days? Thank goodness he wasn't around back when I..." Her sentence trailed off, and she checked her phone.

"Why is there no one here? This won't work if I can't get it done. I can't stay here any longer; it's not safe... darn it!"

Just then, she spotted a man dressed as a watchman coming out of the College and settling into a chair near the gate. Kanak took a deep breath before gathering the courage to approach him. Storing her phone in her back pocket, she wiped her forehead with her palm and cautiously walked towards the watchman. Despite her trembling nerves and thoughts on how to proceed with her plan, the fear of arousing suspicion made her retreat back to her original position.

"I don't know how I'm going to do this, what to say... I can't figure out how to execute this plan. But I have to; otherwise, he might leave, and I'll have to wait again. What if Samrat comes here before me? I'll have to divert them somewhere else before he arrives... yes, that might work. Otherwise, everything will be lost and I can't let it happen."

With a firm resolve, she started walking back toward the watchman and decided to execute her plan. Before she could utter a word, the watchman without even looking at her initiated the conversation, mentioning that admissions had closed with no further opportunities for enrollment.

"I'm not here for admission. I actually want to meet someone," Kanak clarified.

"Who?" the watchman inquired.

"I can't recall the name of the uncle, but he used to work here as a watchman too. He helped my friend Sakshi find a room near the College."

"I don't know any watchman like that, and you don't know his name either."

"Yes, actually he used to help students find places to live near the College, and he also used to take commissions for it. And he helped my friend Sakshi in finding a place close by, and there was this lady, Ahilya, who used to rent out her place for such students."

"I see, but I don't know any of them. But you've given me an idea for a side business," the watchman chuckled.

"What idea?" Kanak asked.

"Helping students in finding places to live near the College and taking commissions for it." The watchman laughed.

"Oh, that!" Kanak laughed.

"Yes, you could do that... Anyhow, I wish I could meet that uncle. I wanted to say thank you after all these years. I'm visiting this place after a long time."

"That's nice."

"Okay then, by the way, thank you for talking to me; it was nice."

"No problem. And thank you for the idea," the watchman laughed again.

After their conversation, Kanak wasted no time and straight away left the place without looking back at him. Her sudden disappearance left the watchman puzzled.

"Who was she? She started asking questions and vanished without even telling me her name. What a peculiar woman." the watchman remarked.

Her attempt to avoid appearing suspicious had clearly failed, and she realized that her swift departure after the conversation with the watchman must have left nothing but fleeting impressions in his mind. As she walked away from the spot, she couldn't help but wonder what the watchman might be pondering about her and what lingering questions might be swirling in his thoughts. Regardless, her focus shifted quickly to her next plan— and so she was concerned about the meeting with the tea stall owner and all she could think about was how to carry that plan along.

"I realize I made a mistake by impulsively bringing up the watchman from my College days, but there was no other opportunity to mention it. Besides, the watchman may have retired by now, and this was the only way to manipulate Samrat and Madhav without even letting them know. It might have made me seem foolish, but dwelling on it won't help. I seriously cannot let myself waste any more time thinking about all the mistakes however I have to be a little more attentive and a bit more careful this time. I must focus on the next step; I can't afford to waste more time fixating on my mistakes. I need to be more attentive and extremely cautious this time. The encounter with the tea stall owner must go perfectly, and I can't afford to raise any suspicions," she contemplated, determined to proceed flawlessly.

As she strolled toward the tea stall, she was preparing herself to have a cautious conversation with the person, and at the same moment, all the while being careful not to attract the attention of Ahilya or her son Madhav, as they reside somewhere nearer to the place. The stall was conveniently located within walking distance of the College, and she was mindful of the need to approach discreetly.

A few minutes later she arrived near the tea stall and watched the tea stall owner across the street. The surroundings felt nostalgic to her. Nostalgia washed over her as memories flooded her mind, evoking both smiles and remorse. The familiar surroundings brought forth a mix of emotions. The gentle breeze that brushed against her skin seemed to carry an unsettling sensation. She stood there for a moment, taking in the sights around her.

"Some things have changed some are still the same. I never thought of visiting this place again but certain things draw you back to your ill."

Kanak reflected with a deep breath as she approached the tea stall owner. As she arrived, she noticed two customers seated on the bench, enjoying their tea. Nostalgic 90s songs played softly in the background from a phone placed near the stove, and the owner attentively poured tea into a cup.

"Excuse me," Kanak addressed him, adjusting her voice.

"Yes, madam?" the owner replied.

"Do you know a woman named Ahilya? I believe she resides around here."

"What's happening... everyone seems interested in Ahilya, madam."

"What do you mean?"

"Well, a few days ago, a police officer came asking about her, and then another one inquired about her, and now you. Did she do something?"

"No, actually, there used to be a girl named Sakshi who lived with her as her tenant."

"Yes, yes, there were some girls who lived there; she always had tenants. But after that accident, everything changed."

"Okay, I mean I just know that there used to be this girl named Sakshi with her and she used to study at the College... K.M College."

"Okay, okay... Actually, Ahilya madam had two girls as her tenants last time..."

"No, I mean, it's a little difficult to... to have two tenants, you know. I think she had just one," she interjected.

"There were two. I remember it clearly."

"Do you happen to know her?"

"I don't know, madam... And now Ahilya is also not in the condition to keep tenants. By the way, who are you?"

"I'm actually looking for my friend... She mentioned that she was living with a woman named Ahilya."

"Alright, when was the last time she told you? Don't mind, but I mentioned that after an accident, things have changed, so it might have been a long time ago."

"Oh, okay. No problem. Thank you for your help, though."

"But I didn't tell you where Ahilya madam resides... She doesn't live too far. Just go straight and take the second left, and there you will see an old, damaged building. The building opposite to that is where she is currently living."

"Thank you; really good talking to you, and thank you for helping me out," Kanak said, bringing a smile to the tea stall owner's face.

After expressing her gratitude and bidding him farewell, she set off in the direction as per his instructions. Upon reaching the spot where she had to take the left turn, she discreetly hailed a rickshaw and quickly took a seat, concealing herself from the tea stall owner's view.

"To The Good Lounge..." she mentioned the place's name as she sat in the rickshaw.

"Do you have the address? I don't know where that place is" the driver asked.

"Yes, I have. Just head to The Good Lounge," she replied.

CHAPTER 16
THE GOOD LOUNGE

The rickshaw driver brought his vehicle to a halt beside a tree, conveniently close to the address Kanak had provided. He inquired if she wanted him to transport her all the way to her destination, but she politely declined, asking him to stop a short distance from the lounge instead. Stepping out of the rickshaw, she retrieved her wallet from her shoulder purse. It was no ordinary wallet that a woman carried; rather, a man's wallet containing Kanak's identification cards, credit cards, and a sum of money.

As she extracted money from the wallet, the driver couldn't help but cast a curious glance at it, breaking into a smile.

"You carry a man's wallet? That's strange," he remarked casually.

Kanak didn't give any response but continued with her task, delivering the payment to the driver without uttering a word. With that done, she left the place, embarking on a walk towards The Good Lounge, her lodging for the past three days.

During her journey, a maelstrom of thoughts raged within her mind. She grappled with the various actions she had taken in hopes of finding a solution. Yet, an undercurrent of uncertainty tugged at her, making her question the soundness of her plan. Even she herself harbored doubts about its effectiveness, acknowledging the need to seek an alternative path out of her predicament.

The lounge stood as a two-story edifice, featuring a quartet of rooms on its ground floor and an equal number on the upper level. Nestled adjacent to the entrance on the ground floor was a diminutive chamber, tailored to accommodate a sole occupant at any given time. Positioned on the right-hand side of the entrance, this petite enclave was accompanied by a counter that graced the opposite end. Access to the compact room was discreetly granted from a vantage point behind the counter. In contrast, the remaining rooms occupied the expanse to the left, a mere 4 to 5 paces removed from the counter's presence.

Upon her arrival, Kanak adopted a posture of lowered gaze. She forwent the customary exchange of pleasantries, navigating her path toward the designated room. However, just as she embarked on this place, a voice emerged from the vicinity of the counter. The woman standing there called out to her, effectively halting her progress and beckoning her attention from behind.

"Excuse me, madam," the woman's voice rang out, drawing her forth from the concealment of the counter. Kanak came to an abrupt halt, her stance poised, and as she let out a deep, resonating sigh, she pivoted to meet the woman's gaze.

"Madam, I am not one to repeatedly implore," the woman began with an air of measured urgency, stepping through the threshold of frustration. "However, the gravity of the situation is escalating. Today is the fourth day since you have come. Initially, you said that you would be staying for two days, however, this is the fourth day, and still, no conclusion has been reached. I am being respectful, but it appears the time has come to force you."

Kanak's brows furrowed, her inquiry emerging laden with curiosity. "And what sort of recourse are you considering?"

The woman's response followed with exasperation woven into her tone. "I am going to tell my associates, and—"

"And what?" Kanak interjected, her voice infused with chilling resolve.

"Do you suppose I am unaware of your activities? As if I won't tell the police about your pursuits?"

A touch of incredulity crept into the woman's countenance.

"What are you saying? What allegations are these?"

Kanak's lips curved into a sardonic smile, her retort unfurling with calculated precision. "Oh, the inconspicuous camera in my bathroom, nestled beside the faucet, cleverly camouflaged beneath a veneer of cement. Ingenious, if I dare say. Wouldn't you agree?"

A note of protest rose in the woman's voice, laden with denial. "I do not know what you speak, madam."

"No room or bathroom houses a camera, I assure you. This is merely an unfounded assertion. I am cognizant of your motivations. I understand the hesitation to settle your dues has driven you to fabricate such stories. Nevertheless, these claims are false."

"If all these are false, why then does anxiety cling to your demeanor? If your conscience is clear, there shouldn't be any room for nervousness."

"I am neither nervous nor anxious. You, misguided woman, would do well to relinquish my funds and depart from my lounge."

"See, I apologize for not paying my dues. I am prepared to disburse the entirety of your requested sum. I am not interested in anything you do here okay? But please... I promise I will pay your dues before leaving."

"And when might this leaving transpire?"

"I am not aware of the precise timing or day."

"What!"

"However, rest assured, I will pay it."

"No! Your assurances hold no sway with me. Remember, I had previously cautioned you that a failure to meet daily rental obligations would necessitate your departure."

"I did engage to settle the debt; I beseech you, to desist from this incessant barrage of inquiries."

"No! I shall persist in my queries until such time as the rent is rendered."

"Then suit yourself."

Turning her back, Kanak navigated toward her room, situated conveniently adjacent to the stairwell. Taking the keys from her purse, she unlocked the door, granting herself passage into the confines of the room. With a decisive click, the door was locked behind her, ensconcing her within. A sudden eruption of frustration followed as she exclaimed, "Shut up, bitch! Shut up!"

Her brief exchange with the proprietor of The Good Lounge had gradually escalated into a heated dispute. This pattern persisted over the last two days, a direct consequence of her inability to fulfill her financial obligations to the landlady. The stipulation for residents at the lounge mandated a daily rent payment structure. A complete day's stay required the payment of the full rent, while a stay of twelve hours or less incurred a half-rent charge. Even if the stay exceeded twelve hours by a mere one hour, the individual was still liable for the full daily rate. The sum for a full day's stay amounted to three thousand rupees, while a half day's stay demanded fifteen hundred rupees.

Initially, Kanak held the belief that managing her stay in one of these accommodations would be a simple task. She was confident in her ability to handle the situation. However, as she left her parent's house, she was under the impression that she could easily withdraw cash from a nearby ATM if her initial plans didn't pan out. In case that option failed, she planned to use online payment methods to cover her rent. Despite her well-laid plans, none of her strategies yielded positive results, leading her to find herself in the current predicament she was facing.

"Why is everything going against me now? What have I done to deserve this?" Kanak lamented as she sank onto the bed in frustration.

The room she occupied was a compact single-person space. Within its confines, there was a solitary bed, accompanied by a nearby table. On this table rested a tabletop fan. Positioned in front of the bed, a small shelf was affixed to the wall, serving as a repository for clothing. Kanak had placed her bag of garments there. The room featured a window that permitted some light to enter. However, the walls exhibited visible cracks, giving the impression that they could crumble at any moment. Despite the room's dilapidated condition, Kanak was required to pay a sum of six thousand rupees for her stay. If she extended her stay for an additional day, the cost would escalate to nine thousand rupees. Seated on the bed, Kanak set her shoulder bag beside her and began mentally calculating both the accumulated expenses and the remaining payments necessary for her stay in this rundown room.

"I've been here for the past four days, including today. I managed to cover two days' worth of rent, which amounted to six thousand rupees. Now, I'm faced with another six thousand rupees due. This place is draining all my savings, and I don't have enough cash on hand to make the payment. Using my phone for online transactions is risky, as the recipient's name would be visible. This is frustrating! There's no nearby ATM where I can withdraw the money. And why does this place have to be so far from the city? It's as if everything is working against me right now!"

Contemplating her situation, she reclined on the bed and shut her eyes, surrendering herself to the darkness that enveloped her vision. Slowly but surely, she succumbed to sleep.

At seven in the evening, a sudden knock on the door shattered her slumber. The forceful sound of the knock startled Kanak, jolting her awake.

"Who's there?" she inquired.

"Unlock the door, it's me," came the response from the lounge's owner.

"I'll settle the rent payment today. Please don't disturb me," Kanak pleaded.

"Open the door," the owner commanded more forcefully.

Kanak found herself compelled to comply and swung the door ajar. Standing there was a man, accompanied by the owner. The man stood at approximately six feet in height, possessing large round eyes that were shadowed by dark circles. His hair was tied back, and his complexion exhibited a pallor. He was attired in a black shirt and black trousers.

"He will assist you in locating a nearby ATM. Obtain the cash and empty this place by day's end. I'm indifferent to your destination or accommodation – all that matters is that you settle my rent and depart," the owner conveyed sternly.

Kanak chose silence over words and turned to collect her bag of clothes and shoulder bag. She gathered her belongings and followed the man.

Descending the stairs, the man led the procession, with Kanak and the owner following in his wake. Upon reaching the counter, the woman behind it vociferously instructed them to ensure Kanak didn't escape and to ensure her return once the payment was secured. The man acknowledged her directive, motioning for Kanak to lead the way. As they exited the lounge, he guided her to perch on his motorcycle.

"Take a seat; this won't take long," the man assured.

"Fine," she acquiesced.

He settled onto the motorcycle, and right after, Kanak positioned herself behind him. With the engine engaged, he kick-started the vehicle and initiated the journey.

By seven past thirty in the evening, the search for an ATM had commenced. Yet, Kanak, seated behind him, had slipped into a drowsy state. She shielded her face with a scarf as they ventured forward. Passing by several shops, they scoured the area for ATMs, persistently traversing the landscape. After a span of minutes, a much-awaited sight emerged: an ATM positioned beside a shop. The man steered his motorcycle toward the shop and instructed Kanak to disembark.

"Hand over your phone and bags; I'll wait outside," he directed.

"Why? I have no intention of running," she retorted.

"My trust is lacking, and refrain from questioning. Simply follow my instructions. Now, proceed and retrieve the money."

Reluctantly, Kanak surrendered her bags and phone, making her way into the ATM. The man lingered outside, his gaze fixed on her, meticulously observing her every move. From within, Kanak secured the money and displayed it, waving the cash she held in her hand. As she emerged from the

ATM, she allocated some funds into her pocket and proffered the remainder to him.

"Here," she handed over the money.

He returned her belongings, clutching the cash as he positioned himself on the motorcycle. Revving the engine, he embarked on the next leg of their journey.

"Are you leaving me here?" she asked, a trace of uncertainty coloring her voice.

"Yes," he confirmed and accelerated away, leaving Kanak stranded in an unfamiliar location all by herself. And Kanak found herself immobilized, left only to watch him recede into the distance.

CHAPTER 17
BACK TO HOME

Retrieving her phone from the shoulder bag, she unlocked the device and launched the map application, intent on plotting her route back to her home address. Upon entering her home location, the app estimated a thirty-three-minute journey by vehicle. She reasoned that taking a taxi for half the distance and then completing the rest on foot would be her best course of action. With confidence in Samrat's likely absence at this hour, she found solace in the thought that she wouldn't have to face his inquiries immediately. While she anticipated addressing his questions in the morning, her current state of mind sought respite from conversations.

"It's a reasonable choice to opt for a taxi. How absurd, that man's behavior! How could he strand me in this unfamiliar and unknown place, especially at this time?" Her frustration found a voice.

A glance at her phone's screen revealed the time as 8 p.m. Promptly, she began her search for a taxi, moving away from the ATM. Soon enough, she spotted an unoccupied cab.

"Excuse me, would you be able to take me to Jhansi Apartment? I have the address and can give you the directions," she asked the driver.

"Sure," he agreed, and she entered the waiting taxi.

The driver skillfully followed Kanak's instructions, guiding the vehicle for fifteen minutes until they arrived at the destination. Eagerly peering ahead, she confirmed that the apartment matched the specified details. Disembarking, she consulted the driver about the fare and handed him the cash she had withdrawn from the ATM. The exchange resulted in the driver returning her change. Subsequently, she examined the route to her home and commenced walking in that direction.

"I hope Samrat isn't home right now. Facing him in this state at this hour would be difficult. But I'm confident I can navigate his questions tomorrow. I know how to divert his attention... I'm sure he won't harbor any doubts. His trust in me is unwavering. This situation... it's going to make our lives challenging, and I can't afford to lose him or his presence. I'm aware I'm not being fair to him, but this will ultimately resolve everything. The less I remember about those events, the easier it will be for me to move on," she murmured to herself.

After walking for twenty minutes, she drew close to her apartment building. Taking a moment to inhale deeply, she proceeded toward her residence. Upon arrival at her front door, she discovered it securely locked. A sense of relief washed over her, knowing the door was properly secured. Unlocking it, she stepped inside. An unpleasant odor greeted her, but she didn't react with anger. Instead, she smiled, placed her bags on the couch, and headed straight for the kitchen. There, she encountered a stack of unwashed dishes in the sink. Scanning the kitchen for other indications of disruption, she spotted discarded food packaging in the trash, indicating what Samrat had subsisted on during her absence.

Progressing to the bathroom, she confirmed her expectation upon observing his soiled clothes hanging in a corner. Moving into the bedroom, her anticipation manifested into reality. Although the bed was neatly arranged, his scattered clothes littered the surface.

She knew this was how Samrat lived when she was not in the house, although every time when she used to be away from the home for a few days she expected Samrat to be a little responsible for the house and keep it clean, but every time her expectation shattered making her upset and angry at him for not keeping the house clean in her absence, this time it was a different situation. She was not angry, nor did she want to complain about his careless attitude.

Confronted with the sight of disorder, she resolved to restore order within the confines of the house. Stretching her body to its limits, she embarked on her cleaning mission. As the clock ticked past ten in the evening, she initiated her efforts in the bedroom. Sorting through the clothes, she scrutinized each item, discerning the clean from the soiled. Employing her sense of smell, she verified their condition before folding the clean garments neatly, segregating them from the untidy ones. Proceeding to the kitchen, she tackled the accumulation of unwashed utensils. Methodically, she cleansed the stove and the dining table, subsequently arranging the freshly washed utensils in an orderly fashion.

The bathroom was her next destination. Extracting the clothing strewn about the bathroom, she transferred the garments to the waiting washing machine. This included not only the attire from the bathroom but also the untidy clothes previously situated in the bedroom. Filling the machine with water, she introduced washing soda, allowing the clothes to soak for a span of ten minutes. Amid her task, the realization dawned that her own garments required attention. Venturing into the front room, she retrieved her clothes from her bag, integrating them into the load alongside Samrat's apparel. With both bags in hand, she returned to the bedroom, placing them within the confines of the cupboard.

Setting the washing machine in motion, she resolved to address the state of the washroom. Dispensing a cleaning solution, she methodically applied it across the surfaces, initiating the process of cleaning the space into one of cleanliness and order.

Engaged in these domestic tasks, the hours stretched beyond two, and Kanak remained steadfast, her determination unwavering until every chore was meticulously accomplished. With two hours of focused effort behind her, she eventually eased her body onto the couch. Leaning her head back, a yawn escaped her lips, accompanied by a stretch of her tired arms.

"At last, everything is completed. But this lingering odor is still making the house quite insufferable," she noted.

Rising from the couch, she headed to her bedroom in search of a room freshener. Opening her cupboard, she commenced her search by inspecting the contents of one drawer, yet it eluded her. The next drawer yielded no different results. Frustrated but determined, she lowered herself to the ground and explored the depths of the bottom drawer. There, tucked beneath a pile of older clothes, she located the room freshener. However, an unexpected discovery awaited her – a discovery so startling that it propelled her backward, disrupting her balance and sending her to the ground in a tumble.

This unforeseen object was entirely out of place within her home, an occurrence that caught her off guard. At that moment, a strong impulse surged through her, compelling her to incinerate or discard the item. However, she realized that such actions would only raise further suspicions and doubts if noticed.

"What on earth is this doing here? I'm positive I turned that whole place to ashes, so how is this even here?"

It was the book—precisely the same one Samrat had retrieved from the police station among the recovered items. It rested atop the other book he had brought from Ahilya. She gingerly lifted both books from their place, studying them closely.

"Why... how... could this thing possibly be in my house? Has Samrat somehow uncovered the truth behind the fire? Has he unraveled the mystery behind it all? No, that can't be. If he had discovered anything, he would have contacted me. No, nothing has changed. This book holds no power over me. I've carefully orchestrated my plan, and it will unfold as I've designed," she muttered, her anxiety palpable.

Returning the books to their original positions, she closed the drawer and secured the cupboard, finally leaving the room. As she exited, a bead of sweat trickled down her forehead, which she promptly wiped away and thought "No, Nothing will happen, apprehension shall merely pave the way for doubt. And I can't allow it to rule."

Emerging from the bedroom, her thoughts remained fixated on the book and the intricate plan she had set in motion to divert both Samrat and Madhav's attention. In the kitchen, she settled onto a chair, leaning her head against her hand, striving to regain control over her state of mind.

"I can't let Samrat entertain any suspicions about me, and it's just a book after all. It won't lead to anything significant. I'm certain of that. I won't let myself fret over it. Additionally, I must maintain my composure around Samrat – I can't afford to lose my temper, can I? No, I can't. Moreover, the executed plan will effortlessly redirect their focus. Yes, it will. If Madhav inquires at the college or the tea stall about the girl, the watchman, and the owner will confirm the existence of a girl named Sakshi who lived with Ahilya. It's as straightforward as that. But what of Samrat? He's a police officer, and I know he'll probe further, asking questions like 'How do you remember?' or 'Who was she?' or 'Did you gather any leads?' Yet, even then, the truth won't come to light – I've taken precautions, disguising myself completely. Yes, they won't recall who I am, most likely."

As she concluded her thoughts, a trace of hesitation infiltrated her, causing her confidence to waver momentarily. Despite this internal struggle, she persevered in managing her emotions, determined not to betray her concerns.

"Take a deep breath, Kanak. Just relax," she reminded herself, drawing a calming breath.

"Now, all that's left to do is await Samrat's return, prepare a hearty meal for him, and gather information about the progress he's made on the case during my absence," she affirmed, a hint of a smile gracing her lips as she turned her attention to cooking.

Observing the lack of ingredients suitable for cooking, Kanak resolved to make a trip to the market to acquire some fresh vegetables. Retrieving her wallet and phone from the bedroom, she kept both things in her tote bag and exited her apartment, intent on purchasing the necessary supplies.

Upon her return from the market, she first went into the bedroom to keep her bag, then she deliberated over the evening's menu with all the ingredients she had bought. Despite being fully aware of Samrat's anticipated absence for the night, she opted to prepare a meal fit for two. The dishes she assembled were all tailored to Samrat's preferences.

"I can keep them preserved and serve them to him in the morning when he returns," she mused, setting aside his portion and serving herself dinner. The spread included a flavorful chicken gravy, accompanied by rice, and a salad composed of cucumber, onion, tomato, carrot, and beetroot.

"Mmm... I've truly missed this delightful taste," she exclaimed, savoring the initial bite.

Savoring her meal to the utmost, she activated the television and began the search for a movie to accompany her dinner. Once she settled on a choice, she immersed herself in the film's storyline.

With her dinner completed, she set the plate down on the table before the couch and eased herself into its comfort. Resuming her movie, she allowed herself to unwind further, indulging in the narrative and finding genuine enjoyment in the cinematic experience.

Yet, Kanak's behavior reflected an enigmatic disposition. One moment she exhibited tension, haunted by her past, only to shift seamlessly into a state of relaxation and assurance, exuding calm confidence in her ability to manage her circumstances.

However, this sudden alteration in Kanak's demeanor bore an air of uncertainty, casting a shadow that seemed to hint at a looming disaster in her future. Oblivious to the impending storm, her thoughts remained fixated on her devised plan and its successful execution. Driven by her conviction, she believed she possessed the cunning required to outmaneuver anyone, even a seasoned police officer.

At half-past midnight, Kanak closed her eyes, slowly succumbing to slumber, with the television still playing in the background. The ambient noise from the TV didn't intrude on her tranquility as she drifted into a deep sleep.

In her dream, Kanak's brow was damp with sweat as she bore witness to the sight of a person's throat being mercilessly slit. While her eyes remained dry, her expression betrayed a profound sense of shock. Fully aware that any efforts to revive the fallen figure would be futile, she still shook her head, desperate to awaken him, despite the inevitable conclusion that he wouldn't rise to his feet again.

"Lalit... wake up! What have you done, Kanak?" A voice quivered.

"Lalit, what happened... damn it!" the voice quivered again.

"He was acting inappropriately... I had to defend myself..." Kanak said

Breaking her silence, her words spilled out involuntarily, as if recited in her mind before finally finding a voice.

"You've taken his life! He was my most valued customer!" the voice echoed

Abruptly, Kanak awoke, fear etched across her features. A trembling hand reached up to touch her forehead, confirming the presence of perspiration. She drew heavy breaths, her chest heaving, and used a hand to wipe away the dampness.

"Just a nightmare... nothing but a nightmare," she reassured herself aloud.

"Alright, don't worry. What's the time?" She queried, her gaze shifting to the wall-mounted clock. It read two-forty-five. Taking solace in the hour, she tried to quiet her racing thoughts and coax herself back to sleep. However, the persistent drone of the television began to interrupt her once again. Deciding to put an end to the noise, she reached over and switched it off, seeking the solace of slumber once more.

CHAPTER 18
THE BURNT APARTMENT

Upon arriving at the charred apartment in close proximity to Ahilya's residence, Samrat noticed an overwhelming hush prevailing in the surroundings. Turning off the engine of his vehicle, he cautiously peered outside to survey the area. Devoid of any visible individuals, the locale exuded an eerie stillness.

Stepping out of his car, he ensured the door was securely shut, stowing the keys into his front pocket. A quick self-pat down confirmed the presence of his diary and phone—essential things for his investigative venture.

"I'm all set to uncover some clues; hopefully, I won't return empty-handed," he murmured, his gaze sweeping the vicinity.

"Why does this place always maintain such profound silence, as if people here refrain from surrounding beyond their abodes? Well, no matter, I should focus on my work," he remarked, proceeding towards the building and ascending the stairs with assured stride.

The apartment's entrance was positioned next to the staircase, and upon entering, the walls were charred black, revealing the imprints of flames amidst the obscurity of the lingering smoke. This sight wasn't new to Samrat; having been here before, he expected the condition. Familiarity eased his entry, yet this time he was determined to meticulously explore. His focus was unwavering, capturing every detail.

The apartment itself was an abyss of darkness, the only discernible features being some scorched remnants of furniture. Commencing his investigation, his first task was to examine the viewpoint visible from Ahilya's unit. With two rooms at his disposal, he chose the right one, once occupied by Ahilya. Approaching the window, he peered out. Amidst a slightly obscured view, Ahilya was spotted in her bedroom, jotting something down beside the window—an intelligible gesture. After a brief moment, he shifted his attention.

"The place seems to have devolved into destruction, utterly shattered. But how did fire consume this building?" he mused aloud, his hand brushing against the room's fractured and partially collapsed bed. A wooden bookshelf lay fragmented on the floor. Retrieving his phone, Samrat began capturing the scene. The lens first captured the room's window, followed by the damaged bed, then the shattered bookshelf, and finally, the scarred walls. With his visual documentation complete, he exited to explore the adjacent room, previously occupied by Kanak. The adjoining room stood devoid of any furniture or belongings, a fact that caught Samrat's attention with a tinge of bewilderment.

"Why is this room empty? Was it never inhabited?" Samrat's internal monologue pondered aloud. Confusion gnawed at him; both the tea stall owner and Madhav had mentioned that Ahilya shared this space with her tenants. The anomaly sparked a sense of unease within him.

"It's perplexing. According to what I've been told, Ahilya lived here with tenants, yet the room is a blank canvas. There's an unsettling element to this. The apparent accidental fire doesn't sit right with me. This is more than just happenstance; it's as if someone meticulously tried to put this place into destruction. This is no impulsive act; it's a carefully calculated scheme. Something significant transpired within these walls—something dark, concealed, a truth deliberately buried," his thoughts flowed.

Amid the currents of uncertainty swirling within him, he methodically captured images of the adjacent room. His photographic documentation commenced with the walls, followed by a meticulous series of shots showcasing the flooring—three to four angles meticulously frozen in time. The culmination of this visual narrative was an encompassing view of the room, lensed from the vantage point near the entrance. He concluded his investigation for it and exited the space, finding himself at the pivotal nexus of the front room—a strategic location affording a comprehensive view of both adjoining rooms. Seizing this perspective, he captured it through his mobile phone.

Subsequently, he embarked on a measured perambulation within the front room's confines. Within this space, a couch, charred beyond utility, reclined, its sorry state rendering it uninhabitable. An accompanying table, bearing four drawers, exhibited signs of neglect and decay—its frontal aspect marred, seemingly unaltered from its original position.

"I'm confounded," he mused aloud, a contemplative furrow on his brow. "Every piece of furniture within this apartment appears anchored in its designated space, as though the conflagration respected their arrangement." He said keeping his phone in the front pocket of his trousers, its work temporarily concluded.

His index finger grazed the table's corners, dispelling the gathered dust. In a single fluid motion, he tugged the table towards his left, his hand exerting a controlled force. The movement was accompanied by an audible thud, a resonance that suggested an object had shifted in tandem with the table's displacement.

The revelation immediately prompted a cascade of thoughts. Swiftly, his fingers danced across the handles of all four drawers, each inspected meticulously. However, the contents within failed to align with the source of the earlier sound. Perplexity gnawed at him. He stood in contemplation for a moment, musing over the elusive sound that had reached his ears. Having meticulously examined the table's anterior orientation, he then endeavored to effect a subtle adjustment.

With a deliberate shift, the table now occupied a frontal position. As he studied the tableau, a latent detail captured his attention—a keyhole discreetly embedded within the table's design. An exclamation of disbelief escaped his lips, laden with incredulity.

"A keyhole behind the table? What purpose could this feature serve? Concealing something, undoubtedly. Perhaps harboring a secret—I hope there's something," he mused, an undercurrent of optimism pervading his thoughts.

Despite the conspicuous absence of a handle adjoining the keyhole, Samrat was cognizant that the door would likely unlatch itself upon the insertion of the key. However, he resolved to bypass the search for the key, opting instead to employ a cautious approach to dismantle the door. Contemplatively pivoting, he embarked on a quest within the room, seeking an implement with the necessary strength to effect a controlled breach of the door's barrier.

"Damn it!" he ruminated, casting a discerning eye over his surroundings. An impulse surged within him, a realization that his solution might rest within his vehicle.

"Perhaps my car has something," he conjectured, propelled by urgency.

Departing the apartment, his stride quickened as he arrived at his car. Swiftly retrieving the key from his pocket, he unlocked the vehicle and entered, his objective clear: locate a suitable tool within the car's confines. His initial search focused on the storage compartment, yielding no results. Undeterred, his gaze shifted to the rear seat, yet this too yielded no viable instrument.

A fleeting moment of contemplation ensued as he grappled with the dilemma. A surge of determination propelled him to relax his mind and body, a brief respite in the midst of the quest. Emerging from his car empty-handed, he locked it and retraced his steps back to the apartment. Crossing the threshold, he positioned himself near the enigmatic table, absorbing a fortifying breath as a prelude to the next chapter of his exploration.

"I cannot afford further dallying. Time presses and the door must yield," he declared resolutely, his urgency palpable.

The allure of unraveling the enigma within overwhelmed any notion of patience. Placing himself behind the table, he anchored his left hand to its surface, fingers coiled in a steadfast grip. The right hand balled into a forceful fist, a vessel of unrestrained power directed at the door's integrity. With a mighty impact, the door felt the brunt of his intent, the resultant collision birthing a hairline fracture.

Unhesitatingly, he pursued another punch, the door's resistance succumbing to his relentless assault. The fracture widened, revealing a glimpse into the concealed realm beyond. Undeterred by the ache that now punctuated his hand, he shifted his stance, assuming a poised position on his toes. The splintered wood beckoned, a physical barrier to be dismantled.

Methodically, he extracted the remnants of the shattered door, his determination unwavering. In the wake of his actions lay revelations that stoked a tempest of conjecture within him. The tableau before him bore testimony to a camera and an assemblage of photographs. Suspicion interwove with astonishment, a whirlwind of thoughts converging upon Samrat's consciousness. Bruised palm forgotten, his focus narrowed to the camera—a Toshiba Tosner, vintage in its character.

Ascending from his crouched stance, he scrutinized the camera, in an attempt to glean understanding from an unfamiliar artifact. While his grasp of its intricacies remained tenuous, his resolve remained steadfast—to decipher, to unearth the unseen.

"This antiquated camera, nestled here in secrecy—why?" his voice resonated with bewilderment as he meticulously examined the camera. With a deliberate gesture, he accessed the camera's interior, revealing a concealed reel within.

"A reel... I ought to handle this with caution, but the urge to unveil its contents is insurmountable," he deliberated aloud, his tactile exploration halting short of tampering. Resuming his composure, he carefully repositioned the component, leaving it undisturbed on the table.

A perceptive shift led him to the trove of photographs.

"Girls?" he uttered in a tone laced with incredulity.

The captured images portrayed young girls, comfortably seated on a sofa, bearing an air of mutual agreement. Each photograph bore a numeric sequence on its reverse, composed of four digits.

"Four thousand, eight thousand, three—what in the world does this signify?" Frustration punctuated his words as he scrutinized each photograph individually. Unease crept into his voice as he continued, "Why would Ahilya have these young girls as tenants? Please, let this not be true. I hope my fears are unfounded."

The puzzle pieces began to coalesce in his mind. The identical pattern of four-digit markings resonated with his earlier discovery—the enigmatic photograph found within the book. The chilling realization crystallized within him: a haunting suspicion that Ahilya might have been entwined in human trafficking.

"No, I am thinking bullshit... Could it be that the sum she used to collect was, in fact, exorbitant, albeit varying for each tenant? The intention behind these photographs remains elusive—does it mirror her true nature? Regrettably, I can't even ask her anything regarding this she won't remember anything but. But did no one know this? Astonishingly, this seems to be a well-kept secret. None appeared to possess even the faintest inkling. Madhav, perhaps—knows these, the camera. Now, however, is not the opportune moment for such musings. My priority is to locate a proficient cameraperson skilled in vintage equipment. The delicate task of converting the reel into photographs awaits, as does the effort to ascertain if any missing person reports correspond to these girls. I need to work fast on this thing... this is... this is going insane, this mystery of Ahilya is going insane. Unfortunately, this cannot be shared; it would be unwise, at least not without substantial evidence in hand. I ought to amass concrete proofs before broaching this subject with others," such are the thoughts articulated by Samrat.

Midway through his introspective dialogue, an incoming call disrupted his thoughts. Retrieving his phone from his pocket, he scrutinized the caller's identity—his mother-in-law.

"Hello, Samrat," her voice traversed through the device.

"Hello, maa. How are you?" he replied gently

"All's well. And you?" Her query followed suit.

"I'm alright. Is everything fine on your end?" he asked, his curiosity tinged with hope for any mention of Kanak.

"Kanak, how is she? Is she with you?" He probed further.

The unexpected response caused a brief lapse in his words.

"What? I assumed Kanak had returned home by now. It's been four days and she still hasn't made it back?" Her tone carried curiosity.

"Four days?" his voice barely audible, a mixture of realization and concern crept in.

"Hello?"

"Yes, perhaps she's back and I haven't noticed. I'll reach out to her and confirm. I'm currently tied up with work, but I'll update you soon. Please don't worry."

"Alright, do take care, both of you."

"Goodbye, and take care," he concluded before disconnecting, the weight of the situation settling in.

The call concluded, leaving a trail of uncertainty in Samrat's thoughts concerning Kanak's inexplicable four-day absence.

"She wasn't at her mother's place, so where has she been all this time? No calls, no messages. I should call her right away."

His fingers poised over his phone's keypad to dial Kanak's number, but he hesitated midway.

"No, she's not naive. Maybe she sought refuge from her parents' persistent advice, taking a breather somewhere, perhaps at her friend's residence. I'll ask once I get home. She's alright, I'm sure of it," he reassured himself. With that, he gathered the camera from the table, along with the assortment of photos, and exited the apartment.

Emerging onto the staircase, he dialed one of the numbers from his call list and briefed them about the camera's condition. Urgency underlined his request for the photos to be swiftly developed from the reel.

"Meet me at the police station. I'll hand over the equipment. I'll be there shortly."

Concluding the conversation with concise directives, he settled into his car keeping his phone in the right pocket of his pants. Safely stowing the camera and the photos within his car's storage compartment, he ignited the engine and embarked on his journey.

Distracted by a whirlwind of thoughts, Samrat maneuvered his car within the police station's confines. As he brought his vehicle to a halt, he spotted an individual waiting beside a tree. The young man, of modest stature and adorned with a mustache, sported a blue shirt paired with trousers. The sound of the car's engine caught the guy's attention, prompting him to approach the vehicle. His gaze fixed on Samrat, who held a camera in his grasp.

"Hello, sir," the young man greeted respectfully.

Taking a step forward, Samrat handed over the camera, his instructions precise and urgent.

"I need you to develop the photographs from this camera. Make sure you deliver this to me as soon as possible."

The young man accepted the camera, expressing a hint of concern, "Certainly, but I must mention that this might take a while. Given the camera's vintage nature and rarity in modern usage..."

Acknowledging the challenges, Samrat interjected, "I understand the situation. Just do your best to expedite the process."

Handing over the camera, Samrat watched as the young man departed from the police station's premises, his mission now underway. Once the young man was out of sight, Samrat accessed the storage compartment of his car. Retrieving the photographs, he resolved to safeguard them in his desk drawer.

"I must gather more information about these photographs," Samrat contemplated. Clutching one of the photographs, he exited the car and made his way into the police station, where Officer Rao occupied his desk alone.

"Well, well!" Officer Rao's face lit up as he spotted Samrat's arrival.

Samrat responded with a subdued "Hello," his demeanor tinged with disappointment.

Approaching his desk, he skillfully slid open the drawer, stashed the photographs within, and securely locked it. During this process, Officer Rao had keenly observed the photographs in Samrat's possession, his curiosity evident. However, he maintained his dignity and refrained from inquiring about them—an act that garnered Samrat's appreciation. Meanwhile, Samrat, attuned to Officer Rao's restrained behavior, found solace in the absence of probing questions.

Following the placement of the photographs, Samrat consulted his watch; the time read seven minutes past ten. He let out a weary yawn, propping his elbow onto the table and cradling his face in his palm. The allure of a brief reprieve seized him, and he surrendered to the need for rest, allowing sleep to claim him.

CHAPTER 19
SHE'S HOME

His peaceful slumber was abruptly interrupted by the sharp chime of his cell phone emanating from the right pocket of his trousers. The sudden sound jolted Samrat, prompting him to become acutely aware of his disheveled appearance. Swiftly, he sought out a comfortable seated position and cleared the accumulated grit from the corners of his eyes with his bare hands. As he settled, the call was already disconnected.

With practiced swiftness, Samrat retrieved the phone from his pocket, revealing a missed call from Kanak's mother. Waste no time, he promptly returned the call.

Without delay, a voice answered on the other end. "Hello? Maa?" he inquired, his tone tinged with drowsiness.

"Samrat? Have you arrived home safely? Is Kanak there?" The concern in her voice was palpable.

The call regarding Kanak's recent disappearance had slipped Samrat's mind. To him, it represented a significant concern, capable of inducing considerable stress. This situation was not unfamiliar, as Kanak had confided in him on multiple occasions about her tendency to leave her parents' home under the pretext of returning to their own place when in reality, she was visiting a friend. However, the identity of this friend had never been disclosed to Samrat.

He was accustomed to Kanak's mother's unease over her daughter's actions, as he himself understood her perspective. In her eyes, Kanak was perceived as a self-absorbed individual who showed little regard for her parents' feelings and often acted contrary to their wishes. Consequently, after their marriage, it was strongly advised that Kanak share every aspect of her married life. Initially resistant, she eventually acquiesced, turning this counsel into an implicit directive she was obliged to follow.

In the early years of his marriage, Samrat found this ambiguous demand from his mother-in-law disconcerting. However, with time, he integrated it into his routine, in deference to Kanak.

"She will be fine, try not to fret too much. Have you attempted calling her?" Samrat reassured.

"She's not picking up," she replied with concern.

"Have you had any disagreements recently?" he inquired.

"No," she asserted.

"Alright, don't let it trouble you. I'll return home and update you shortly," he promised.

"She has never acted this way before. Please, take care of her," she implored, her voice strained.

"Naturally, mother. She's my wife, and it's not the first time..." he trailed off, choosing not to finish the sentence.

"You need not worry, alright?" he reassured, his tone steady and comforting.

After the conversation, he placed the phone on the table and ran his fingers through his hair, contemplating whether he should call Kanak to ascertain her whereabouts. However, Kanak's words echoed in his mind, dissuading him from entertaining the idea. Taking hold of the newspaper with one hand, he motioned to a constable to fetch him a cup of tea.

"Hurry, please. It feels like my head is on the verge of exploding with all of this," he requested.

"But sir, it's rather late, and there won't be any tea stalls open at this hour," the constable informed him.

"What's the time?" Samrat inquired, consulting his wristwatch. It read nine minutes past fifty. He conceded that it was indeed too late for a cup of tea.

"Sir, I think you should head home and get some rest. You appear quite fatigued," the constable advised.

"I am weary, but returning home will only agitate me further," he admitted.

Turning his attention to the newspaper, he immersed himself in its contents. After a few minutes, he could feel Officer Rao's gaze directed at him. Though he initially resisted engaging in conversation, his fixed gaze eventually compelled him to break the silence.

"Could you please refrain from staring at me?" Samrat requested, folding the newspaper and placing it on the table.

"I'm simply pondering something," he replied.

"Cease the staring and do your pondering elsewhere."

"I've always been cordial with you, yet you consistently respond with hostility. Why?" Officer Rao questioned.

"Hostility? I'm not a hound to bark at you. Frankly, I find our conversations distasteful. I go out of my way to avoid you, and you're well aware of the reason, yet you choose to take offense," Samrat retorted.

"I'm attempting to mend our relationship, alright? You needn't be so abrasive every time we speak."

"I have no interest in reconciling with you. I've moved on, and your words hold no sway over me," Samrat asserted.

"Samrat..." Officer Rao began, pausing briefly before continuing, "Holding onto grudges will only weigh you down. It's better to let things settle."

"I've learned from my past," Samrat maintained.

"I don't harbor any grudges. I simply don't want us to revert to our old ways. I can't trust you anymore," he concluded.

Listening to Samrat's words, Officer Rao's expression turned inscrutable. He had nothing further to add, only offering a nod of agreement.

At four in the morning, Samrat meticulously gathered his belongings - his phone, car keys, and apartment key - stowing them away in the left pocket of his trousers. He double-checked the drawer to ensure it was securely locked before making the decision to head home. Approaching his car, he deftly inserted the key into the lock, swung open the door, settled into the driver's seat, and fastened his seatbelt. With a turn of the key, the engine hummed to life, and he set off toward his residence. The crisp breeze filtering through the car window brushed against his face, causing his eyes to water. He dabbed them gently and stifled a yawn, eager to reach his destination.

Arriving at his apartment complex, he slid the key into the lock and noticed Kanak's sandals by the entrance, a telltale sign that she was home. A smile crept across his face. He kicked off his shoes and ventured inside to find her, discovering her serenely slumbering on the couch, completely lost in her sleep. On the table, he spotted unwashed dishes. He gathered them up, proceeding to the kitchen to place them in the sink. As he entered, he was met with a pristine space - all utensils had been thoroughly cleaned and properly arranged, the sink gleamed, and there was no lingering scent of food. She must have tidied up, he mused.

Knowing that Kanak had prepared a meal, he opened the refrigerator to investigate. Inside, he discovered a steel pot containing chicken gravy, complemented by a vibrant salad of cucumber, onion, tomato, carrot, and beetroot neatly arranged on a plate. He retrieved the pot and plate, setting them on the table beside a medium-sized bowl of cooked rice. After washing his hands, he took a seat, and with care, began to serve himself.

Savoring each delectable bite, he made a deliberate effort to consume his meal in absolute silence, mindful of not disturbing his wife's peaceful slumber. As he relished the flavors, his thoughts delved into the events of the prior day. He contemplated the photographs and the camera he had stumbled upon in Ahilya's former apartment. His mind replayed the conversation with his mother-in-law about Kanak's presence at home.

Suddenly, Kanak entered the kitchen, rubbing her weary eyes. Observing Samrat quietly enjoying the meal she had prepared the night before, she noted that he remained oblivious to her arrival, providing her the opportunity to initiate a conversation.

"You're here," she remarked, taking a seat across from Samrat.

He snapped out of his contemplative reverie, finding Kanak seated before him.

"I was about to say the same," he replied.

"I hope you won't repeat that behavior," she cautioned.

"Mom called me twice, worried about your whereabouts. Where were you?" he inquired.

"You know how she can be—" Kanak began.

"You weren't answering her calls, and she sounded quite distressed. What were you up to, and where were you?" Samrat pressed.

"You're aware that I get frustrated with my parents and occasionally spend time with my friend. I've explained this to you before, Samrat. Why are you asking me as if I've been deceiving you?" Kanak retorted.

"I never accused you of lying, Kanak. I simply didn't know where you were, and you instructed me not to contact you. Your anger frustrates me, Kanak. I really dislike this side of you. You disappeared without a word and told me not to reach out. Do you think that's fair? It's not," he voiced his frustration, a mixture of anger and sadness evident in his tone.

"I won't let you vanish like that again. I won't permit you to go anywhere, even if we argue," he asserted.

"What did Mom say?" Kanak asked, her focus shifting to the part of his statement concerning her mother's inquiries.

"She asked if you had returned home. I know you get upset, but I'm not comfortable with you staying with your friend. Who is this friend?" Samrat inquired.

"Why?" she asked, her response swift.

"Are you doubting me?" she questioned once more.

"Why do you always assume that? I'm simply asking about your friend," he clarified.

"It's nothing."

"Kanak, I've never pried into your affairs—where you go, what you do. But this time, I felt genuinely uneasy about not knowing anything. If something had happened to you, what would I have done? You're my wife, and I want to be more attentive to you."

"Nothing is wrong; Mom tends to overreact. I'll give her a call and set things straight. Don't worry. Now, finish your meal," she reassured.

"Kanak, please," he insisted.

"Samrat, you really don't need to worry, okay?"

"I just want to know who your friend is, at least her name," he questioned her, pushing his plate forward.

"What did Mom say to you? Did she say something wrong?" he asked.

"Nothing," she said, averting her gaze from Samrat's face.

"Then tell me, what's your friend's name?"

"Samrat..."

"Kanak, please tell me the name. I'm not asking for anything else. A husband should at least know his wife's friends," he pressed.

"Why does it feel like you are questioning my absence? You never asked before about my friend, then what happened this time?" she tried to deflect his questions by asking some of her own, for she didn't want to answer Samrat's question. After all, Kanak never had any friends. Since her college days, she never tended to make friends. She believed that having friends meant taking care of their needs and sharing emotions with them, and Kanak seldom shared her emotions with others. Also, her behavior never inclined her to be friendly with anyone during her college days, hence she never pursued it. She did try to be friends with Ahilya, who shared the same sense of knowledge as Kanak, but that part of the friendship became a nightmare for her. Since then, Kanak had no friends.

"Sakshi, alright? Her name is Sakshi."

No other name came to her mind, and she felt foolish for choosing that one.

"Okay, thanks," he replied.

She tried to mask her hesitation after mentioning the name and asked, "Thanks?"

"For coming back."

"I always come back to you."

"But why do you leave? Never leave again," he implored.

Their conversation concluded as Samrat finished his meal, placing the utensils in the sink. By seven o'clock in the morning, they both retired to bed. Although Kanak suggested he should rest alone, asserting she already had a full night's sleep, Samrat insisted on having her by his side. He yearned to be close to his wife.

CHAPTER 20
THE GIRL NAMED 'SAKSHI'

At nine in the morning, Samrat slumbered deeply, while Kanak, restless, chose not to join him in sleep. Instead, she lay beside him, mulling over Samrat's revelations about her mother. Regret gnawed at her for uttering the name 'Sakshi'. Perhaps it had surfaced due to her preoccupation with it in recent days, she surmised. But confessing it to her husband had been an error, one she couldn't undo. She had no other schemes in motion; that was the solitary plan she'd conceived. When Samrat inevitably questioned her about 'Sakshi,' she'd need a different false explanation. Yet, no plausible response came to mind, nothing that could mislead him. She continued to ponder, her thoughts in a whirl until she felt Samrat's hand gently graze her belly.

"Don't dwell too much on Mom," Samrat murmured, his voice drowsy.

Turning to face him, Kanak met his serene countenance with a steady gaze. She realized her thoughts had been too vocal and, with a tender touch, brushed her fingers against his lips before planting a gentle kiss. At the touch of her lips, Samrat drew her closer, initiating a fervent kiss.

"I've missed you terribly," he confessed amidst their embrace.

"I understand," she responded, though her sentiments didn't mirror his. She hadn't yearned for him, hadn't harbored the same feelings he did, for she was cognizant of the complexities he wasn't.

"I'll freshen up," she stated, easing herself slightly away from him.

"No," he protested, pulling her back. "Stay, I want you near. Let's linger like this a while longer."

"Aren't you headed to the police station?"

"I'll give it a miss today."

"Just a little while longer, alright? Then I'll go get ready."

"Of course, baby. Mind if I join you?"

"Sure, if you'd like."

He smiled and drew the blanket over both of them, cocooning them from head to toe.

At half past ten in the morning, Kanak's thoughts still circled around the name that had slipped from her lips while she prepared breakfast for herself and Samrat. She couldn't afford to reveal her inner turmoil and uncertainty to her husband, yet, at the same time, she couldn't conjure up an alternative strategy to sidestep this situation. And so, she decided to let time work its course. Lost in her contemplations, she failed to notice Samrat standing beside her, filling a glass with water. He bestowed a smile and a kiss upon her shoulder.

"You're up? Planning to go out?" she inquired, glancing at Samrat, who was not attired in his usual home attire.

"Yes, but don't worry, I'll be back in an hour," he reassured.

Curiosity flitted across her mind. Where could he be off to, she wondered.

"Alright, have breakfast before you leave," she advised.

"Will do," he concurred.

Samrat pulled up in Ahilya's neighborhood, parking his car in front of the tea stall. He figured this visit wouldn't take up much of his time, and he was eager to return home to his wife.

"Any updates for me?" he inquired as he settled onto the bench.

Earlier in the day, around ten in the morning, his phone had rung from an unfamiliar number. Still groggy from sleep, he hadn't bothered to check the caller's ID.

"Hello, who's this?"

"It's Mohan, from the tea stall, sir. You asked me to inform you about anything related to Madam Ahilya."

"Ah, yes... What have you got?" Samrat replied, rubbing the sleep from the corners of his eyes.

"I can't discuss this over the phone, sir. Could you please come to my stall?"

"Alright, but it had better be worthwhile to make me travel."

"It's crucial, sir."

"If I find this information unhelpful—"

"Yesterday, a lady came here. It was in the afternoon. She was asking about Madam Ahilya."

"A woman?"

"Yes. I didn't pay much attention, as I was quite occupied. She had a handbag slung over her shoulder, and she wore a mask. One thing she mentioned was a girl named Sakshi, looking for someone who used to reside with Madam Ahilya."

"Sakshi?"

"Yes."

"And anything else?"

"She mentioned the girl used to study at K.M College. If you inquire with the college's watchman, he might have some information. He's been there for a good ten years now."

"Did you notice anything peculiar about the woman asking about Ahilya? Any details that stood out?"

"One thing did strike me as odd. She asked for Madam Ahilya, but I hadn't told her where Madam lived. Still, she thanked me and was about to leave. It was as if she didn't care to know the exact location."

"Hmm, peculiar indeed," Samrat mused.

From Mohan's account, Samrat extracted three key pieces of information: Sakshi, the woman, and K.M College. Finishing his tea, he handed the glass back to the stall owner.

"Thank you for sharing this. Stay in touch, alright?"

"Sir, I've helped in this case. I believe a tip would be in order, considering my circumstances—"

Samrat preempted him by handing over a five hundred rupee note.

"Keep this. I knew you'd bring this up, which is why you called me here."

"I have a family too, sir."

"Indeed, you do."

With a parting smile, the owner bid Samrat farewell. Samrat chose not to engage in any debate over the money, valuing the pursuit of further leads over any potential ethical dilemmas. However, a nagging thought lingered about whether this could be construed as bribery. His focus now honed in on K.M College, the girl, and the long-serving watchman.

Samrat's initial priority was to locate the watchman at K.M College. According to the tea stall owner, the college was close by, and the watchman who had been on duty during those years was still the same. It seemed plausible that he could provide information about the girl named Sakshi. However, if the watchman struggled to recollect, that could pose a challenge. Nevertheless, Samrat decided it was worth a shot.

He started the engine, following the GPS directions on his phone. The distance was 2.3 kilometers, estimated to take approximately seven minutes. Samrat navigated the route as instructed: first, a straight stretch of 350 meters, then a right turn at the junction, followed by another 700 meters in a straight line, and finally, a right turn at the signal.

Soon, he arrived near the college. It was a bustling weekday, teeming with students. Samrat parked his car to the left of the college gate. Scanning the surroundings, he spotted a figure seated on a chair nearby. Judging by his appearance, Samrat surmised that this could be the watchman. The man, in his sixties, wore a blue shirt and navy trousers, neatly tucked in. Sweat glistened on his forehead.

Samrat thought it might be a good idea to offer him some water. Retrieving a half-filled bottle from the back seat of his car, he approached the watchman.

"You're sweating quite a bit. Please, have some water," he offered.

The watchman regarded Samrat for a few moments, then accepted the bottle gratefully. He was clearly parched.

"Who are you?" he inquired.

"I'm Samrat, a police officer," Samrat replied, pulling out his identification from his pocket and displaying it.

The watchman rose, though hesitantly. He was unsure why the police were interested in him. He felt a twinge of apprehension but concealed it well.

"What's the matter, sir? Is something wrong?" the watchman asked.

"For how long have you been working as a watchman here?" Samrat queried.

"It's been around twelve years now."

"Do you know Ahilya? Ahilya Mathur?"

"Yes, Ahilya madam. I used to assist in finding tenants for her. Her place isn't far from the college, so many female students used to rent her apartment. She also charged lower fees for girls. However, after an incident, her apartment burned down, and she lost all her memories. Now she lives with her son."

"You used to find tenants for her? Then you must have gathered their information as well."

"Actually, sir..." he hesitated, "my role was solely to help girl students view the place and introduce them to Madam Ahilya. All other details were her responsibility, so I never collected information from any tenant."

"Hmm. Do you recall a girl named Sakshi? She used to be one of her tenants. Do you remember anything about her? She was a student here about eight years ago."

"Sorry, sir. That's quite a long time, and this is a college where many girls with the name 'Sakshi' may have been admitted. But, sir, a woman came by yesterday, I believe. She also mentioned the name 'Sakshi.' She didn't speak with me directly; someone else was on duty in my place that day. Shall I call him?"

"Yes, please do."

The watchman retrieved his phone from his pocket and dialed a number. After a few seconds, the call was picked up, and he put it on loudspeaker.

"Hello, Santosh? You mentioned that a woman came asking for me. And she mentioned the name 'Sakshi'?"

"Yes, what's the matter?"

"Can you describe her appearance?" Samrat inquired.

"Who are you?"

"Answer his question; he's a policeman."

"Sorry, sir. She was wearing a mask, and she had a handbag. She struck me as a bit odd because she didn't provide her name. She left immediately after I mentioned that I didn't recognize any watchman by that description."

"By what description?"

"She said that he used to take a commission from students to show them the place. And yes, she mentioned that the girl named Sakshi was her friend."

"Friend?"

"Yes."

The term 'friend' struck a chord with Samrat. He immediately recalled that Kanak also had a friend named Sakshi.

"Alright, you can hang up now," the watchman signaled to Samrat, asking for permission to end the call.

Samrat agreed, and the call was concluded. Who is this woman? Samrat wondered.

"You used to take a commission?" Samrat inquired of the watchman.

He smiled and nodded. However, for now, that wasn't Samrat's primary concern. He was keen to learn more about this girl Sakshi. Since she had been a student at this college, there must be records about her. Samrat was determined to connect the dots, and with this momentum, he ventured inside the college, seeking out the registrar's office.

The college complex comprised four buildings, each boasting five floors. Within these structures were six spacious rooms, each capable of accommodating at least seventy students. Excluding these four edifices, the college campus extended across ten acres. These buildings were neatly aligned in a circular formation. The structure nearest to the entrance housed the registrar's office, which Samrat easily located. Situated on the ground floor, the office door was shut. Samrat entered without knocking.

The room was sizable, with three elongated tables placed along three sides of the walls. Each table was equipped with two desktop computers and flanked by various files. In the center stood an average-sized table, presumably reserved for the staff's meal breaks, he mused. As he stepped in, he spotted one man engrossed in his work at a desk; besides him, the room was unoccupied.

"Yes? What can I do for you?" the man inquired curtly. He was a stocky figure wearing glasses.

Samrat produced his identification and presented it to the man. The latter promptly rose from his seat, offering a slightly odd smile, evidently mistaking Samrat for a parent of one of the students.

"I need information regarding a girl named Sakshi. She was a student here about eight years ago. Can you assist me with that?" Samrat asked politely.

"Sir, we are not permitted to divulge any student information—"

"I understand, but this conversation stays between us, alright? Rest assured, nothing untoward will occur."

"But, sir—"

"I assure you, there will be no repercussions. Don't worry."

The man started the search by inputting the name and providing additional information, such as the eight-year period. In the meantime, Samrat surveyed the room and decided to break the silence.

"Why are you here all alone? Where's everyone else?" he inquired.

"They've gone for a stroll," he responded slowly.

"And you didn't join them for a walk?"

"No, not at this time. Students often come looking for assistance, so I can't leave the place unattended."

"What's your name?"

"Yash. Yash Sharma."

"Alright, Yash, you seem quite anxious. Rest assured, I won't reveal your name to anyone."

"I'm worried about someone questioning me about why I'm helping you."

"Just tell them I'm your friend who dropped by to see you if anyone inquires. Although I hope this won't take too long. How much more time?"

"Here," he swiveled the desktop screen towards Samrat.

Displayed was a roster of students bearing the name 'Sakshi.' There were a total of five entries, indicating five students with that name. Samrat carefully scrolled through the list, examining the details. Soon, he spotted a familiar face, one he recognized from the photographs found in Ahilya's old apartment.

Samrat focused intently on the screen, striving for a clear view of the photo. The face struck a chord of recognition within him; he was certain he had encountered it in one of the photographs.

"Could these specifics be relayed through WhatsApp?" he inquired.

"Sir, regrettably, that would go against our college's policy. I'm afraid I can't disclose any particulars," Yash replied firmly.

"Well, Yash, correct?" Samrat began, attempting to persuade. "I want to reassure you that this will be handled discreetly. I sincerely hope you'll consider my request, as I'm approaching this matter with utmost courtesy. I trust you'll collaborate with me."

"Okay," Yash acquiesced.

Yash sensed Samrat's patience waning. Realizing that further insistence on the policy could lead to a problematic situation for himself, he consented to share the details. He converted the information into a portable document format and transmitted it to Samrat through WhatsApp.

"I now have your contact. I might require your assistance again in the future," Samrat mentioned, tucking the phone away.

"Understood," Yash replied, acknowledging everything that Samrat said.

CHAPTER 21
THE OVERTURNING

Samrat pressed the doorbell of his apartment and patiently waited for Kanak to answer. As she swung open the door, she immediately sensed the tension etched across her husband's face. She suspected it was connected to Ahilya's case, and though she was eager to inquire, she also hoped Samrat would broach the topic first. After setting his phone and car keys on the table, he sank onto the couch, with Kanak settling beside him.

"You mentioned you'd be back soon," she gently reminded.

"Sorry, I got caught up," Samrat replied.

"In what?" she probed, masking her curiosity.

"It's related to Ahilya's case. I'm convinced there's something significant about it, and I've unearthed evidence that supports this belief. Yet, despite having so much right in front of me, it feels like I'm still missing a crucial piece," Samrat confided.

"Have you made any discoveries?" she asked, her curiosity thinly veiled.

"While you were away, I visited Ahilya's former apartment. I came across some photographs there. Then, this morning, I received a call—it was a lead in Ahilya's case. A girl named Sakshi used to reside with her. So, I decided to check the college's database for her, and sure enough, I found her. Among those photographs, I also found one of her. It leaves me wondering, why Ahilya has pictures of the girls who lived in her apartment. The odd part is that these photographs were tucked away in the back of a cupboard. Can you believe it?" Samrat recounted the entire sequence of events to Kanak, his voice steady and composed.

He turned to study his wife's expression before continuing, "By the way, you also have a friend named Sakshi, right? Do you happen to have any pictures of her? It would be helpful in confirming if she's the same Sakshi I'm looking for."

"I don't have any photos of her," she replied straightforwardly.

"That's peculiar. Women often take pictures of their friends. It's a bit unusual, you know," he chuckled awkwardly.

"I'm not really into taking photos. I'm sorry, I can't be of much help," she explained.

"Come on, don't apologize. Let's not dwell on it. What did you cook?" he redirected the conversation.

"Just a regular meal."

"Alright, let's dig in then. I'm famished."

Samrat started to rise, but Kanak halted him with a gentle grip on his hand, motioning for him to stay seated.

"What's wrong?" he asked.

"I don't know, it just feels a bit strange. I'm scared."

"Why? Did something go wrong?" concern filled Samrat's voice as he observed his wife's somber expression.

"It's as if this Ahilya's case is pulling us apart, and eventually, you'll leave me. I don't want that to happen, Samrat."

"Nothing like that will ever happen. Don't worry, I'm always here for you. Even if the whole world turns against you, you'll always find me by your side. Always," he reassured, cradling her face in his hands and offering her a soothing smile.

His words brought a sense of peace to Kanak, though his final sentence left her with lingering thoughts. "Even if the universe goes against you, you will still find me on your side. What does he mean by this?" she pondered. She held him close, but her mind continued to grapple with Samrat's words.

"Can I eat you?" Samrat unexpectedly queried.

Kanak momentarily grappled with her husband's request, her expression a canvas of confusion. Upon seeing her, Samrat broke into a smile.

"I'm famished, and I'm craving something truly delightful. So, may I eat you?"

"Your moods do shift in the blink of an eye, Samrat."

He chuckled.

"I can't quite grasp what's going on. All I know is, I don't want you to leave again."

"And I won't, as long as you won't let me."

"You're exquisite," Samrat complimented, gazing at his wife's enchanting visage as if beholding the most precious treasure. He leaned in slowly, tenderly brushing his lips against hers. She welcomed his touch, gradually melting into his embrace.

In the evening, Samrat reclined on the couch, engrossed in the television, while Kanak prepared a cup of tea for him. This had become a routine for the past week, as he spent his evenings and nights at home, reconnecting with his wife. He couldn't shake the feeling that his preoccupation with the Ahilya case had been the catalyst for Kanak's temporary departure from their home. He had needed a brief respite from the investigation, even though it wasn't a complete hiatus; he still made regular calls to the person responsible for developing the photographs and checked in with the tea stall owner to see if the same woman who had inquired again about Ahilya.

Suddenly, the thought of calling Kanak's mother and providing an update on their situation crossed Samrat's mind. He wanted to reassure her that everything was going well, and Kanak was in good spirits. He realized that he hadn't spoken to her since that day, but he assumed that Kanak must have filled her in on the details. His phone was in the bedroom, charging, so he decided to use Kanak's phone. As he began to dial the number, a notification popped up on Kanak's screen, prompting her to leave a review on a place she had recently visited according to Google Maps. This unexpected message gave Samrat pause.

Intrigued, he decided to explore the map application to see where Kanak had been. To his understanding, Kanak had been staying with her parents and then relocated to a friend's house—a residence located in the same vicinity as her parents, just an hour's drive away. However, the location indicated by the notification suggested she was near their apartment. Digging further, he checked the application's history and discovered that Kanak had been at a place approximately thirty-three minutes away from their apartment.

"What was she doing there? She wasn't with her friend," Samrat pondered. Doubt began to creep into his mind, prompting him to check Kanak's phone. He decided to examine her call logs, hoping to find some answers. Navigating to the speed dial, he scrolled through to see if Kanak had contacted her friend Sakshi. However, there was no record of such a call. He then checked her contacts list but found no entries under the name Sakshi.

"Did she lie to me?" Samrat questioned, his voice barely above a whisper. He meticulously combed through Kanak's phone, inspecting her photos, and WhatsApp messages, and eventually delving into her SMS. There, he stumbled upon a message indicating a withdrawal of ten thousand rupees in cash.

As Samrat processed the information he had gleaned from her phone, Kanak returned with two cups of tea and set them on the table.

"Here you go," she offered one to Samrat, noticing her phone in his hand. Her surprise was palpable, realizing that the screen was unlocked.

"What are you doing with my phone?" She asked tentatively.

"Kanak, did you lie to me?" he inquired, his gaze fixed on the screen.

"About what?"

"About your friend and your whereabouts, and the money you withdrew. What's all this?" he pressed, his tone resolute, still not meeting her eyes.

"Are you doubting me again, Samrat?"

"Kanak, let's not deflect from the question. Just give me the answers," he finally turned to face her, his stare ice-cold.

"What do you want to know?" She asked, taking a seat beside him.

"Let's start from the beginning. You weren't with your parents, and you weren't with your friend, Sakshi, am I right?"

"I can explain..."

"Am I right?" he raised his voice slightly, unsettling Kanak.

"I wasn't with her."

"Then?"

"I can't tell you. I'm sorry I lied, but I can't disclose where I was. I don't think it's important for you to know."

"But why? You're acting strangely. First, you wouldn't tell me your friend's name, and now you're saying you weren't at her house. So, where were you, Kanak?"

"I don't remember."

"Seriously? That's your excuse?"

"Why did you withdraw ten thousand rupees?" he pressed again.

"Are you really asking me this? Just because I took some cash?"

"Don't be naive, Kanak. I've never objected to you using money, but this time it's different. I want to know why you needed it."

"I don't remember."

"Kanak! Stop saying that."

"Stop doubting me!"

"Then tell me what's happening!"

"I can't tell you, Samrat, but please believe me. I'll fix everything. Please, trust me," she implored, her eyes welling with tears.

Her tears brought a hush over the room, and Samrat's anger gradually began to ebb.

"I genuinely want to know what's troubling you, baby. I want to help. Can you trust me enough to share?" he urged.

"I'm sorry, Samrat, but please believe me. I'll set things right. Can you do that?"

Samrat gently set the phone aside and quietly retreated to his bedroom, opting not to respond to her inquiry. His hope of finding answers from Kanak had been dashed, and seeing her in tears, he chose not to press the matter any further. Kanak trailed after him, acutely aware that she had wounded Samrat and feeling helpless about how to mend the rift. As she entered the room, she discovered Samrat engrossed in his phone. When he noticed Kanak's presence, he spoke, his tone resolute, "I'm heading to the police station and won't be back tonight. Please don't wait up for me."

"Samrat, please don't leave like this. Just try to understand, please."

"Are you understanding me, Kanak? My own wife has been living somewhere without a word to me. Can you imagine how uncertain that feels for me?"

"I promised I'll sort it out."

"Then at least tell me what needs fixing... I want to know what's troubling you, baby. Since you've returned, something's felt off. You keep saying you'll fix everything, but I don't know what's broken. What is it?"

"Samrat..." Her voice quivered as tears streamed down her cheeks.

"Please don't cry, Kanak. Please. It feels like you're pushing me away by keeping things from me. I want to help."

"I can't tell you... not now."

"Then I'll wait for that day, and I hope it comes soon."

Samrat changed into fresh clothes, grabbed his car keys and phone, and left the place.

CHAPTER 22
THE PHOTOGRAPHS

Parking his car in close proximity to the police station, Samrat deftly dialed a number as he emerged from his vehicle. The phone emitted a series of rings, each one carrying a measure of anticipation. Samrat patiently waited for the recipient to answer before proceeding to the station. After a brief pause, the call was answered by the person he had apprised of the photo development.

"Any updates on the photos?" Samrat inquired, his curiosity piqued.

"Yes, I was just about to notify you. They're ready," came the prompt response.

"Kindly arrange for them to be delivered today. I'm eager to review them."

"Understood. I'll be at the police station by nine o'clock. Will that work for you?"

"Perfect. Just give me a call; there's no need to come inside."

"Alright," the person concurred before ending the call.

Samrat found solace in the knowledge that the photo development had reached its conclusion, and soon he would have them in his possession. Nevertheless, the disconcerting thought of his wife's possible deception lingered in his mind. As he stepped into the police station and took his seat, two distinct threads wove through his thoughts: the photograph of Sakshi, concealed in his desk drawer, and the intricate details of Kanak's recent whereabouts.

Upon receiving the notification and realizing that Kanak had been less than truthful, he promptly stored the details on his phone. This way, he could delve deeper into the location and gain insight into the surroundings. His curiosity burned to understand his wife's purpose for being there and why she chose to keep it hidden from him.

After dispatching the information, he removed the message from Kanak's end, utilizing WhatsApp's feature to maintain his discretion. He was aware that Kanak would remain unaware of his acquisition of the location details. With this task completed, he retreated to the bedroom to securely save the newfound information on his phone.

Unearthing Kanak's deception took precedence, compelling him to scrutinize the location through his digital device. Navigating to the application where the message resided, he was seamlessly redirected to the maps interface, revealing the precise location. He zoomed in, scouring the screen for any trace of an ATM, driven by the inkling that perhaps his wife had made a withdrawal there, though the purpose remained elusive. After a deliberate sweep from left to right, he finally spotted the ATM's position, a pivotal discovery that heightened his eagerness to visit the site. He resolved to do so the following day.

Next on his agenda was the photograph. He unlocked the drawer, carefully extracting the images and arranging them in a row on the table. Simultaneously, he accessed the document forwarded by Yash, the acquaintance he had encountered in the college's registrar's office. As he scrutinized the images side by side, it became unequivocally clear that one of them depicted Sakshi.

Within the provided information, Samrat unearthed Sakshi's residential address, her contact number, and her parents' phone details. Armed with this data, he knew it was a gamble, acknowledging the possibility that circumstances might have altered—Sakshi's residence might have changed, or the contact numbers might be outdated. Still, he was willing to take the chance.

"I hope this yields something significant for the case. Heaven only knows what's going on," Samrat mused, exhaling deeply. He initiated the call, dialing Sakshi's number. The line, however, turned out to be defunct, dashing his initial hope.

"This number doesn't seem to exist. Alright, let's try the other one."

He proceeded to dial the number belonging to Sakshi's parents. After a brief pause, the phone rang, eliciting a sigh of gratification from Samrat. A man, sounding elderly, answered after two rings.

"Hello?"

"Is this Mahesh Sawant?" Samrat inquired, his gaze fixed on the screen.

"Yes, who's speaking?" the man responded.

"I'm Officer Samrat Chauhan. I was hoping to gather some information about your daughter, Sakshi. Is she available?"

"Sakshi passed away four years ago."

"Oh, may I ask how? Only if you're comfortable sharing."

"It was an accident. Why do you ask? Is something amiss?"

"No, sir. Everything's fine. I was just interested in learning a bit about her college days. Could you please provide your current address? It would be very helpful."

"Of course."

The man relayed the address, confirming it matched the one in the provided details, indicating that they hadn't relocated.

"Thank you, sir. Take care." Samrat concluded the call.

At eight-fifty in the evening, Samrat's phone rang, the caller identified as Radhe.

"Yes?" Samrat answered, projecting the tone of an on-duty officer.

"Sir, I apologize for not getting in touch earlier. I was dealing with some family matters and didn't find the time. Also, you hadn't called to inquire about the individual you asked me to monitor."

"Who?"

"Madhav."

Samrat suddenly realized he had completely overlooked him. He had questioned Madhav about his relationship with Ahilya some time ago at a café, but Madhav's evasive responses had raised suspicions, prompting Samrat to assign someone to keep tabs on him.

"Yes, he slipped my mind. Tell me, what have you discovered?"

"I delved into his background and learned that he's Ahilya's adopted child. After growing up, he went abroad for further studies, leaving his elderly mother alone. However, the circumstances of his departure were suspicious."

"In what way?"

"After his father's demise, his mother was isolated. The funds from the apartment weren't enough to meet her needs. Money wasn't her only desire either; she started involving herself with other men, becoming intimate with them. That's why Madhav distanced himself from her."

Samrat processed this information for a moment, partly aware of the situation but not privy to the full truth until now.

"Are you certain your information is accurate?"

"One hundred percent, sir. I never provide false information."

"Alright."

The call ended, leaving Samrat with a multitude of questions swirling in his mind. Madhav's reason for distancing himself from his mother had cast a shadow of suspicion over both him and Ahilya. Gradually, the puzzle pieces were falling into place, drawing Samrat deeper into this pool of enigmatic connections.

"Why do I have this nagging feeling that this case is leading to a concealed, larger mess? The photos of the girls, Ahilya's involvement with them, and now this revelation—they all seem to intertwine somewhere. But why did she witness a man's death? Who is that mysterious figure she saw perish? Her husband? Her lover? Or someone else she was entangled with?"

Samrat's mind raced with myriad thoughts, each twist in the case leading him down a new path, somehow tethered to the past. He recalled Madhav's revelation about leaving his mother, but never could he have foreseen this—a mother resorting to such measures for her own satisfaction. It was beyond his imagination, yet undeniably true.

Lost in contemplation, Samrat momentarily forgot about the impending delivery of the photographs due by nine o'clock. He retrieved his phone to make the call, but before he could, it rang on its own.

"I was just about to call you. Please wait outside," Samrat instructed, stepping out of the police station.

The man stood beneath a tree in the darkness. Samrat approached him and received the package—a modest-sized envelope containing the photographs. He handed over the payment and returned inside. Seated, he carefully extracted each of the thirteen photographs, examining them one by one. His hand froze as he gazed upon one image that left him utterly bewildered. He couldn't tear his eyes away, his mind struggling to find certainty in the face before him. It was Kanak, his wife, captured in a moment of radiant smile.

CHAPTER 23
CONNECTING THE DOTS

"Kanak?" Samrat exclaimed, his voice tinged with surprise. The sight of his wife's photograph amidst the others was difficult for him to comprehend. This unexpected twist in Ahilya's case left him in disbelief.

The words that escaped Samrat's lips were barely audible, meant for his ears alone. He fixed his gaze on the photograph, his fingers gripping it tightly. It was evident that there was a connection between Kanak and this case. Samrat had come to realize this, though he knew it was too early to confront his wife. Patience wore thin in his mind, the urge to approach Kanak and unravel the truth was overpowering.

He questioned why Kanak had kept all this from him. Why hadn't she mentioned Ahilya when he first introduced her to the case, or even when he introduced her to Ahilya and Madhav at the restaurant? The notion that Kanak had concealed so much from him left him feeling uneasy and suffocated. This unexpected twist in the case, compounded by Kanak's involvement, had rattled him. He was determined to unearth the truth as swiftly as possible.

Although uncertainty lingered after discovering his wife's photographs, a thought began to form in Samrat's mind regarding all the images he had uncovered. "Perhaps I should consult the department's database on missing persons' reports from the past decade. There might be something that sheds light on these photographs," he mused.

However, conducting this research would require a concerted effort, and it would be more efficient with additional assistance. Samrat scanned the room for a potential ally, someone who could lend a hand without prying or causing further concern. He found no one except Officer Rao in the station. While seeking his help was a slight inconvenience for Samrat, he knew that refusing it would only prolong the process of unraveling the mystery behind the photographs. With little choice, he mustered the courage to approach him.

"Officer Rao, I need your help with something," Samrat asked with hesitation.

Officer Rao was working on one of the files.

"On what?"

Samrat placed the photographs in front of him, except Kanak's photograph.

"I want to check whether our police station had missing complaints filed about this girl. I mean not recently, it's over ten years ago. Can you help me in looking for those files?" Samrat was direct in his favor.

"Okay."

It was a surprise for Samrat to see Officer Rao accepting his demand without asking any questions or making any comments. For Samrat, it was a convenient situation as well.

"Officer Rao," Samrat began, his tone marked with a hint of uncertainty.

Officer Rao was engrossed in a file, glancing up inquisitively. "What is it?"

Samrat placed a stack of photographs before him, deliberately omitting Kanak's.

"I need to ascertain if our station received any missing person reports matching this girl, but from over a decade ago. Can you assist me in locating those files?" Samrat's request was straightforward.

"Alright," came Rao's prompt reply, surprising Samrat with his lack of probing questions or comments. It was a favorable turn of events for Samrat.

In the storage room, silence enveloped them as they methodically sifted through files stacked atop one another. The absence of conversation was a curious deviation for Samrat, who noted Rao's uncharacteristic reticence. They systematically examined records dating back fifteen years, with Rao's careful planning leading the way. Since Samrat lacked specific information about the age of the photos or the year of the missing report, he provided an approximate timeframe of fifteen years, which Rao used as a starting point.

"As you mentioned around fifteen years, let's focus on 2008 and 2009," Rao suggested.

"Alright."

"And if we don't find anything there, we'll move on to 2010 and 2011, understood?"

"Of course."

This was the extent of their exchange before commencing their search. They meticulously combed through files about missing person reports from 2008 and 2009, yet nothing piqued their interest. As planned, they then delved into records from 2010 and 2011. It wasn't until Officer Rao broke the silence, asking, "Is everything alright? You seem a bit concerned about something," that their quiet pursuit was interrupted.

Samrat hadn't realized his apprehension was so palpable, etched across his face for anyone to discern. "No, I'm fine. Why do you ask?" he replied, averting his gaze.

"It's as if you're disappointed by something, but that's never been the case in this investigation. You've never shown disappointment before."

"It's something else."

"Alright," Rao paused, then continued, "I believe I've found one. Can you show me the pictures?"

Samrat presented the photographs, and Rao meticulously compared them, eventually matching one with a missing person report from 2011. The girl's name was Riddhi, and the report included her contact information, address, and guardian's phone number. Samrat documented every detail on his phone.

"Perhaps we should explore further in 2011; there may be more cases like these," Officer Rao suggested.

They proceeded to investigate in 2011, uncovering another photograph that corresponded to those found in Ahilya's old apartment. The second girl was Zoya. Samrat diligently captured all pertinent details from Zoya's file. Among thirteen girls, they had identified two. They followed this pattern, progressing to 2012 and 2013.

After reviewing all the files from 2013, Samrat decided to halt the process. He recollected that Ahilya had been diagnosed with amnesia roughly eight years prior, which meant there wouldn't be any cases filed after 2013 that matched the photographs. They then reverted to years predating 2008.

Over two hours had elapsed, the passage of time unnoticed in their focused pursuit. Eventually, they agreed to conclude their search. By the end, they had gathered details on six girls: Riddhi, Zoya, Mayra, Tashi, Aarya, and Divya. Samrat meticulously recorded all the information on his phone.

At half-past ten in the morning, Samrat sat in his car, discreetly tucked away at a corner of the street. This was the exact location he had pinpointed from the notification on Kanak's phone. His mind was a whirlwind of thoughts, each one a puzzle piece he struggled to fit together. It wasn't that he found them inherently difficult to comprehend, but rather that Kanak's involvement with Ahilya had added a layer of complexity to the situation.

In his mind, he'd concocted a narrative: Ahilya, gripped by loneliness, sought companionship, eventually spiraling into a dark path, turning to prostitution and exploiting the young girls residing in her place as unwitting tenants. Their parents had lodged complaints, yet locating any of these girls seemed a futile endeavor. Somewhere in this web of secrets, either the tea stall owner or the watchman held crucial knowledge. Yet, Kanak's presence in this tale remained a confounding enigma.

Samrat's inquiry led him to a pivotal question involving Kanak. In order to truly grasp her role in this, he decided to visit the same location his wife had been to a few days prior. He approached the locals, inquiring about the nearest ATM. Given that Kanak had withdrawn ten thousand rupees from the bank, he assumed there must be an ATM nearby. After a short drive, he located one.

Stepping out of his car, he surveyed the surroundings, considering that if Kanak had visited this ATM, she likely spent some of the money in the vicinity. Samrat resolved to visit each shop in the vicinity, showing Kanak's photograph. However, her face had been obscured by a scarf at the time, making recognition a challenge.

It was the fourth shop he entered, hoping the owner might have seen someone resembling Kanak.

"Excuse me," Samrat greeted upon entering the grocery store.

The owner glanced up, inquiring, "Yes?"

"Have you come across this woman around here, about four or five days ago?"

The owner studied the photo before responding, "No, I don't think so."

"Are you certain?"

"Yes, quite certain."

"Alright, can you recall any woman or any unusual incident near the ATM? Anything at all, even the smallest detail?" Samrat probed.

The owner recollected, "Well, there was a woman with a man on a motorcycle. They entered the ATM; she emerged with money, and then the man left her near the ATM."

At the very moment when Kanak was handing over the money for the lounge's rent, the shop owner was outside, tending to his storefront. Though she hadn't noticed him, he glanced at the man accompanying her and immediately recognized him.

"Did you see her face?"

"No, but I recognize the man."

"Excellent! Who was he?"

"There's a lounge a short distance away, The Good Lounge, yes... he's associated with it. I know him because the owner of that lounge is a friend of mine," he confessed with a somewhat sheepish smile.

It took Samrat ten minutes to reach The Good Lounge. Upon arrival, he parked his car in front of the entrance. The owner rushed out, clearly agitated by the noise of the car, and upon seeing it obstructing the entrance, she erupted in anger.

"Excuse me, remove your car from my entrance! This is not a parking area. Move!"

"Could you please lower your voice? I'm a police officer," Samrat calmly stated, presenting his identification.

The woman's demeanor abruptly shifted to one of deference.

"I'm sorry, sir. But I'm constantly dealing with people who..."

"It's alright. Do you recognize this woman? Did she stay at your lounge?" Samrat inquired, displaying a picture of Kanak and scanning his surroundings.

"Yes, sir. She was here a few days ago, and I must say it was quite exasperating. She hadn't paid her rent, so I instructed my brother to accompany her to the ATM to withdraw the cash. That's all. Am I in any danger, sir? Did she do something?"

"That's enough."

"So she did stay here, and without cash, she withdrew money from an ATM," Samrat mused.

"Did you notice anything out of the ordinary? Or anything unusual that you recall?" he pressed.

"I can't say for sure, but one day she left while talking on the phone and mentioned something about a 'college,' yes, that's it."

"Alright, can you show me her entries?"

"Yes."

The owner retrieved the logbook from the counter, flipping through the pages until she reached Kanak's entries, recorded under the name 'Anaya.' She presented the logbook to Samrat.

"Anaya," he repeated.

"Yes, she claimed her name was Anaya."

Samrat discreetly photographed the entries in the book before leaving the premises.

Anxiety and confusion swirled within Samrat over his wife's behavior. His primary focus now was to meet Kanak and have all his doubts dispelled. This could only happen if Kanak provided truthful answers without further deception or evasion, and without posing questions of her own.

"But why was she keeping this from me? What was she hiding?" Samrat pondered.

As he approached his apartment building, he mulled over the idea of confronting Kanak about her time at the lounge and her secrecy. However, his own mind supplied the answer: Kanak rarely responded candidly to his questions. Instead, she tended to sidestep them with evasive or untrue replies. This behavior wasn't new to Samrat, and it had led him to avoid situations where he sought answers that Kanak avoided providing. This time, though, the situation was different. It involved something crucial that Samrat couldn't ignore, nor allow Kanak to evade. But was this the right moment to broach the subject? Probably not, he concluded. He deliberated on what else he could focus on.

His thoughts shifted to the progress in Ahilya's case. Madhav emerged as the prime suspect, the watchman potentially entangled in the human trafficking operation leads to the families of missing girls, and a tea stall owner who may be presenting a facade. Of utmost importance was Ahilya.

Given the substantial leads, Samrat leaned towards prioritizing Madhav's interrogation.

"He hasn't disclosed anything about this. Why?" Samrat muttered to himself.

"I understand that confronting Kanak is paramount, but I also realize it would be premature without concrete evidence. I must approach her with a clear mind."

Setting aside his thoughts about Kanak, he proceeded with Madhav's interrogation.

CHAPTER 24
MADHAV'S CONFESSION

Upon arriving at Ahilya's apartment, Samrat remained in the car momentarily, assembling a series of questions for Madhav, anticipating their forthcoming encounter. This set encompassed inquiries regarding information Madhav had previously shared with Samrat, as well as those pertaining to the missing girls, Ahilya's well-being, and the vivid images of the murder that Ahilya was experiencing. Satisfied with his preparation, he exited the vehicle and approached the building.

Recalling that Ahilya's residence was on the floor above Madhav's, Samrat headed first to Madhav's apartment. He found the door securely fastened from the inside. Samrat pressed the doorbell button and waited, allowing a few seconds for Madhav to respond. However, to his surprise, it was Ahilya who opened the door.

"Hello," she greeted with a radiant smile, showing no recognition of Samrat. Furthermore, he was not in uniform. The door was only partially ajar, revealing half of Ahilya's face.

"Hello ma'am, are you here?" he inquired, a hint of uncertainty in his voice.

"Who are you?" she asked, her tone laced with skepticism.

"Could you please get Madhav for me? I need to speak with him," he replied, tactfully sidestepping her question.

Ahilya turned and called for Madhav. "Someone is asking for you. He didn't tell me his name."

"I'll check, maa. Please go back inside and sit," Madhav responded from within. Ahilya left the door slightly ajar and retreated inside.

Madhav returned, opening the door fully to find Samrat waiting outside. "Officer?" he greeted a touch of hesitation in his voice.

"Have you discovered anything?" Samrat inquired.

"May I come in first?" Samrat asked politely.

"Yes, of course."

Following Madhav, Samrat entered the apartment and settled onto the couch beside Ahilya, who was engrossed in the television.

"Have you discovered anything?" Madhav queried once more.

"Yes, a few leads that could potentially shake up this case," Samrat replied.

"Good news indeed. Have you identified the perpetrator?" Madhav inquired.

"Not yet. Actually, I wanted to discuss a few matters with you. Gain some insights from your perspective," Samrat explained.

"My perspective? Sure, go ahead."

"May I trouble you for a glass of water?" Samrat politely requested.

Madhav nodded and started towards the kitchen. However, he was intercepted by Samrat midway, who turned to Ahilya for assistance.

"Ma'am, could you bring me a glass of water?"

"Of course," she replied.

As Ahilya headed into the kitchen, Samrat seized the opportunity to elucidate the need for a private conversation with Madhav, emphasizing that involving any other parties might impede the interrogation.

"I'd prefer it to be a one-on-one conversation," Samrat clarified.

Madhav readily concurred. When Ahilya returned with the glass of water, Madhav chose not to divulge the situation to her, instead suggesting they go to her apartment under a pretext.

"Ma, how about we go out for lunch today?"

"Alright, but who's this gentleman?" Ahilya inquired.

"He's a friend of mine. I'll explain later. Go get ready; we'll be leaving shortly. I won't keep you waiting," Madhav assured her.

He accompanied Ahilya to her apartment and left a note on the table, bearing a message that read 'going out for lunch with Madhav'.

"I know you might not recall, so I've left this note," he murmured, securing it in place.

"I'll be back, ma."

He exited her apartment and returned to his own, where Samrat awaited their private discussion.

"What do you want to ask?" Madhav inquired, noticing the half-empty glass of water. Samrat had taken a sip.

"Would you please share the details of your relationship with Ahilya? I'm interested in knowing how you first met her," Samrat requested.

"I've already told you..."

"I'm not here as a friend, so please cooperate. I only need your account. Please refrain from countering with your own questions, or else we may have to involve the police, and I'm certain we're not ready for that yet."

"Alright. I met her when I was a child. She and my father, whom I used to call Baba, first came to the orphanage, and from there, they adopted me as their child."

"What was the name of the orphanage?"

"It's called 'We are a Family Orphanage House.' It's located outside of this town, in Bangalore."

"Alright," Samrat replied, jotting down the name of the orphanage in his diary. He was already prepared with his notebook and pen when Madhav took Ahilya to her apartment.

"When you were adopted, did you notice anything suspicious about Ahilya or her husband? Anything you can recall?"

"No, she was always kind, protective, and very appreciative. I remember once Baba scolded me for something, and she stopped him. She always loved me like her own child."

"Was she content in her marriage? What was her husband's name?"

"Maa loved Baba wholeheartedly, and he felt the same for her. They were very happy together. However, over time, Maa started becoming conscious about her appearance, and it made her upset. Baba, on the other hand, loved her just the way she was. He adored her."

"Your Baba, what was his name?"

"Ajit. His name was Ajit."

Samrat made a note of every crucial detail as per his assessment.

"Why are you asking me all this? Is it related to the case?"

"Yes, I want to understand the kind of woman your Maa was."

"What?"

"You mentioned that after your father's passing, she changed, and her behavior wasn't good, which is why you left her."

"Yes."

"Is that so?"

"What do you mean?"

"I'm already familiar with the situation and your reason for leaving your mother. However, I'm seeking your perspective. Can you please tell me?"

"You already know... Fine," Madhav chuckled.

"She turned to prostitution. Started selling her body for money and her own gratification. I told her I didn't need money for my education, but that wasn't her only reason. She began to find pleasure in it, she said."

"How did she end up in this situation?"

"I have limited knowledge about it, except for one night when I found her with a guy. I don't recall his name clearly, perhaps it was Lalit. I'm not sure. I confronted her about it, and she confessed that she was involved in this and didn't want to quit. I thought if I could persuade her to leave, she might eventually escape this situation. But that guy exerted pressure and manipulation to the point where she wasn't willing to break free. So, I made the painful decision to leave her and never return. Fate had other plans, you see. I encountered her in the hospital, fighting for her life. That very day, I got the news that the apartment where my mother stayed had burned down, and yes, that guy, Lalit, or whatever his name was, he vanished since then."

"You mentioned a call from a girl."

"Yes, she phoned me and informed me about my mother's condition."

"Why did you keep your mother's... situation hidden? It could have aided me earlier."

"I'm sorry, officer. You see, no one around here knows about my mother's circumstances, and I didn't want any misconceptions about her."

"Madhav, your mother was not only involved in prostitution, but she was also part of human trafficking."

"What?" Madhav was taken aback by Samrat's words. He was grappling with the reality that was painting a picture of his mother he had never believed before. He was struggling to process it.

"No, what you just said can't be true. I know she was involved in prostitution, but she would never do such a thing. I mean this?" He was reluctant to accept Samrat's words.

"It's true. A few days ago, I went to her old apartment, the one she claimed a man was dying in. I searched through everything and found some photographs of girls. I cross-referenced them with the police department's database, and these are the girls whose missing reports were filed."

Madhav couldn't bring himself to accept Samrat's statement. He started shaking his head in disagreement.

"No, officer, that can't be true."

"I comprehend your feelings, but you must understand, I'm merely drawing a potential link here. I haven't imposed any conclusions or declared it as fact, alright? I may be mistaken, so I implore you to work with me on this."

"Take a look at these photographs. See if any of them seem familiar."

Samrat had taken pictures of the photographs on his phone before leaving the police station. He showed them to Madhav.

"No, I don't remember seeing any of them. After that incident, I never really visited my mother. Like I told you, after all those years, I met her in the hospital. In that condition," Madhav replied, handing the phone back to Samrat.

"Alright," Samrat said, stowing his phone in his pocket.

"Samrat... About the human trafficking, are you certain? Do you have any evidence?"

"I'm not making any definitive claims, nor am I saying it's confirmed. But I have suspicions about your mother's involvement, based on these photographs and the missing reports."

"Yeah, I can't wrap my head around this. It's truly devastating."

"I'm sorry, man. Well, I know it might sound selfish, but can you do something for me? I understand your mother's condition, that she likely doesn't remember anything. But I want you to try asking her about this Lalit guy. There's a chance she might recall something, maybe."

"Of course."

"Could you do it now? I have a lot on my plate."

"Oka--"

"Please call her here," Samrat interjected, not allowing Madhav to finish his sentence.

Madhav picked up his phone from the table in front of Samrat and dialed Ahilya's number. The phone began to ring.

"Hello, Madhav?" Ahilya's voice came through.

"Maa..." he replied somberly.

"Can you come to my place?" he asked.

"Were you ready for lunch? I was waiting for your call."

"Please come to my apartment."

He ended the call, and both of them waited for Ahilya to arrive at the apartment.

A knock on the door signaled Ahilya's arrival. Madhav went to open it. She stood outside with the note he had written about lunch in her hand.

"Who is he?" Ahilya inquired upon seeing Samrat seated on the couch.

"A friend."

"Alright. Shall we go? Are you joining us, son?" she asked Samrat.

"Maa... I'd like to ask you something. Please try to remember, okay? Do you know anyone named Lalit? Does that name ring a bell?"

"Lalit?" she mumbled, her expression turning sorrowful.

"Lalit... wake up!" she suddenly cried out. "Wake up, he's dead, she killed him!" she began to shout and then collapsed to the ground.

Samrat swiftly rose from his seat and rushed to hold Ahilya.

"Who killed him?" he inquired urgently.

Madhav carefully carried Ahilya back to the couch and helped her sit.

"Maa, calm down. Do you remember him? Who is he?" Madhav tried to console her.

Ahilya started to weep.

"Lalit, my love... she killed him..."

CHAPTER 25
THE FINAL CONNECTION

Upon witnessing Ahilya's visceral response upon hearing the name 'Lalit', Samrat was solidified in his belief that the man she described in her harrowing account of the burnt apartment was none other than Lalit. This revelation casts a new light on the complex web of relationships: Lalit, once Ahilya's paramour, seemed to have been intricately involved in the enigmatic circumstances, as per Madhav's cryptic allusions.

However, Samrat found himself in a conundrum. With no discernible leads, and Ahilya's emotional state rendering her unapproachable on the matter, he was left grappling with yet another critical piece of the puzzle that lacked a clear trail to follow. Yet, amid this frustrating impasse, Samrat clung to a reservoir of information that held the potential to steer the investigation toward a conclusion. Thus, he resolved to temporarily set Lalit aside, focusing instead on the other available threads.

His anticipation mounted as he awaited the receptionist's report on the patient in question, Ahilya Mathur, diagnosed with Amnesia. The computer whirred for a few moments, sifting through data spanning nearly a decade.

"Is it ready?" he inquired, his curiosity palpable.

"Yes, sir," the receptionist responded, her tone polite but tinged with a hint of trepidation.

"Please, share the particulars."

"Um... certainly, but I implore you to keep my name out of this, sir."

"You have my assurance."

With precision, the receptionist produced a printout, passing it over to Samrat. His gaze traversed the lines of text, revealing Ahilya's history of Amnesia and her prolonged stay in the hospital. He neatly folded the document into a compact square, tucking it into the recesses of his jacket.

"Does Doctor Jagdish Shekhawat still practice here?" Samrat inquired, swiveling towards the receptionist, his eyes locking onto hers.

Dr. Jagdish Shekhawat had been instrumental in Ahilya's care during her hospitalization, as attested by Madhav. His expertise and efforts had garnered high praise not only from Madhav but from the entire staff, establishing him as a luminary within the hospital's medical fraternity.

"Yes, he maintains a presence, though his visits are limited to Thursdays."

"Thursdays, I see. What day is it today?"

"Saturday, sir."

"No matter. Could I trouble you for his address? It would be of immense help, and I assure you, there will be no repercussions."

"Sir..." the receptionist hesitated momentarily, letting out a sigh.

She extracted the address from the computer, committing it to paper before presenting it to Samrat.

"Here."

"Thank you. By the way, I neglected to ask for your name."

"Shreya... Shreya Sane."

"Much obliged, Shreya. Your cooperation is greatly valued."

With resolve, Samrat set forth to meet Dr. Shekhawat, wasting no time in transitioning to his next destination. He settled into his car, extracted his phone, and keyed in the address. The estimated travel time flashed—fifteen minutes. With a purposeful ignition, he embarked on the path ahead.

In under fifteen minutes, he arrived at his destination. As he rapped on the door, his gaze swept across the surroundings—an independent dwelling, much like the others in the vicinity. The street buzzed with the spirited activity of children engaged in a game of cricket. After three brisk knocks, the door swung open, revealing a woman on the other side.

"Is Doctor Jagdish Shekhawat at home?" Samrat inquired.

"Yes, and you are?" the woman responded, adjusting her attire.

"I'm Officer Samrat. I'd like to speak with Doctor Jagdish. Could you please fetch him?"

"Ah, alright. Just give me a moment. Please, come inside. Would you like a glass of water or anything else?" she offered.

"No, just Doctor Jagdish will do," Samrat replied with a smile.

The woman retreated indoors and tapped on the door, leading to the doctor's bedroom. It remained locked from within.

"He'll be out in a moment. Please, have a seat," she said, gesturing for Samrat to sit.

"May I ask who you are?" Samrat inquired.

"I'm his housekeeper. Actually, the doctor lives here alone."

"No spouse or children?"

"He never married."

"And how long have you been working for him?"

"It's been a year. He's quite absent-minded."

"Do you reside here too?"

"No, my shift ends at seven in the evening."

Shortly thereafter, Doctor Jagdish emerged from the room—a septuagenarian, his hair a brilliant white, countenance etched with lines of time, yet he carried himself with the posture of a much younger man.

"Hello there," the doctor greeted, extending his hand for a shake.

Samrat reciprocated the gesture and exchanged pleasantries.

"Am I in some sort of trouble?" the doctor inquired.

"No, Doctor. I simply have a few questions pertaining to one of your patients."

"Ah, which one would that be?"

"Ahilya Mathur. I trust you recall her?"

"Oh, I could never forget her, I'm quite certain. What do you need to know?"

"When she was initially admitted, can you recall who brought her in?"

"A young lady, if memory serves... yes, it was a young lady. She not only admitted Ahilya but also completed all the necessary paperwork."

"Do you happen to know her name?"

"Her name was Sakshi."

As Samrat jotted down notes, his hand momentarily stilled upon hearing the name.

"Are you absolutely sure?" he inquired, a trace of skepticism in his voice.

"Without a doubt. Typically, people are anxious or perturbed when they bring someone to the hospital, but this young lady displayed none of that. She was composed, collected, and alert. And she was wearing a mask."

"But how could you discern this if you didn't see her face?"

"Her demeanor, her voice, her movements—everything seemed rehearsed as if she had prepared for this situation in advance. I involved the police in the case as well."

"Then what happened?"

"Then, I got word that Ahilya's residence had gone up in flames, taking all the evidence with it. I believe the police failed to take adequate measures in tracking down the culprit."

"And what about that girl? Did she return?" Samrat inquired, pen poised over his notepad.

"No, she never came back. It was a couple of days later when Ahilya's son showed up. She had lost her memory, unable to recognize her own flesh and blood. It was truly heart-wrenching to witness that boy struggle to restore his mother's recollections. She could only recall fragments, mostly the perilous chapters of her past. There were nights when she'd peer out the window and weep, and she'd speak of a man... I can't recall much, just bits I overheard from the staff. Her condition was exceedingly rare; she suffered from both retrograde and anterograde amnesia. Those with retrograde amnesia struggle to recall past memories, while those with anterograde find it challenging to form new ones. In Ahilya's case, she grappled with both, and she continues to do so today."

"Yes."

"Is something amiss with her?"

"No, I've just learned some particulars about her in my pursuit of clues. Anyway, do you recall anything out of the ordinary with her, or anything that raised suspicions?"

"No, nothing of the sort. Once her son arrived, everything seemed to normalize. May I ask what's going on?"

"Ahilya claims she witnessed a man's demise in her former apartment. She would scream and gesture towards the window of her previous abode."

"It could be a fragment of her past that refuses to fade, but she's unable to discern the exact details of that scene. There's a possibility that such an incident actually occurred."

"It's entirely possible."

While they conversed, the woman had quietly exited the room and busied herself in the doctor's bedroom, tending to the bed and organizing his attire.

"You have a housekeeper. She informed me that you've never married."

"I never had the opportunity. The demands of my career and my patients kept me too preoccupied to entertain thoughts of marriage."

"Do you ever contemplate it now?"

"Well, I do regret not leading a conventional life like others, but presently isn't the time to grant that thought much weight."

"Understood. Thank you, doctor. I trust you have a pleasant day."

As Samrat ignited the engine of his car, his thoughts revolved around the name the doctor had mentioned.

"The doctor brought up Sakshi, Ahilya mentioned a girl, Madhav spoke of a girl who informed him about Ahilya's hospitalization, and even the tea stall owner and the watchman referenced a girl. But who is she? It can't be Sakshi, as Sakshi is no longer alive. Ahilya used to have tenants, and according to the tea stall owner, there were two last time. It's possible that one of them was Sakshi, and the other could be an imposter using her name. I must uncover her identity."

That evening, upon his return home, Samrat discovered Kanak waiting for him in the front room. It had become a routine for her to anticipate his arrival and attempt to soothe him regarding the matters she had kept concealed. Meanwhile, Samrat harbored a sense of discontent. His wife had begun to withhold information from him, and the suspicion stemming from her stay at the Good Lounge had triggered a host of unspoken inquiries in his mind.

Samrat entered the bedroom in silence and began to pack his clothes into a bag. Kanak followed him, hesitating.

"Are you going somewhere?" she asked.

"Yes, for a day or two."

"Where?"

"That's not important. I'll be back by tomorrow night, don't worry."

"Samrat... there's something I need to tell you. It's important."

"My work is important too, so I'll listen to you once I return."

"Samrat..."

"Kanak, not today."

"Can you at least tell me the destination?"

"I'm heading to Gujarat. It's for a case."

Samrat's train to Surat was delayed by thirty minutes. He waited at the station, perched on a bench. Sleep eluded him, knowing the train could arrive at any moment. To stay awake, he opted for an energy drink. The journey to Surat was estimated to take around three hours, which meant Samrat would need to spend the night at a hotel before proceeding to Sakshi's house. The address he had for Sakshi's house was a forty-minute drive from the Surat station. Samrat had already reserved a room in a hotel closer to Sakshi's residence.

After downing his energy drink, Samrat grabbed a quick snack. Finally, he saw the indicator signaling the arrival of his train. He boarded and took his seat, preparing for the journey ahead.

By twelve-fifteen in the early morning, the train pulled into the Surat station. It was late at night, no transportation services were readily available to take Samrat to his hotel, even after presenting his credentials. He sought out a cab to book, but none were accessible.

"Is there any service that can take me to Hotel Stay Inn?" Samrat inquired with one of the cab drivers.

"At this hour, I doubt you'll find any cabs," the driver replied.

"I'm willing to pay double. Just take me to that hotel. How much does it usually cost?"

"Normally it's two hundred for the special seat. But at this hour, I can help you for five hundred."

"Alright."

"You have the address, right?"

"Yes, I have it. I'll guide you with the directions."

"Okay then."

After twenty-five minutes of driving, Samrat arrived at the hotel. He provided his details and completed the check-in process. Once inside his room, he did nothing more than lie down on the bed. Grasping the cushion beneath his head, he closed his eyes and gradually drifted off to sleep.

On this scorching day in town, Samrat took a sip of water, feeling the beads of sweat forming on his skin. Sakshi's parents observed him closely.

"The heat can be quite relentless here," he remarked.

"Yes," agreed Sakshi's father.

"I won't take up much of your time. I just need to gather a few details about Sakshi and her college days," Samrat explained, jotting down notes in his compact diary.

"Of course," Sakshi's father replied.

"Where did Sakshi last attend college?" Samrat inquired, his pen poised.

"She was pursuing her Masters at K.M College in Mumbai. She was residing as a tenant in someone's apartment," he supplied.

"Do you recall the name of her landlady? Did she ever mention anything about her?" Samrat probed.

"Yes, she used to mention her, but not in a favorable light. She complained about her being strict and rude," Sakshi's father recalled.

"I see. It appears she wasn't fond of her landlady, Ahilya."

"Perhaps."

"Did she share anything else about her college or her friends?" Samrat turned to Sakshi's mother.

"To me, not much. Sakshi was a cheerful soul. She captured moments with her camera, every occasion, every place, everyone she met, and anyone who became her friend. She was quite outgoing. During her college days, she spoke about her friends, her studies, and her living situation," Sakshi's mother reminisced.

"Can you recall anything unusual or noteworthy? Any particular incident she mentioned?" Samrat inquired.

"Well, she once told me that she wasn't happy with her landlady because of her strictness and rudeness towards her," she began.

"And?" prodded Samrat.

"So, she made the decision to change her residence and moved in with a girl from her class."

"Did she elaborate on any specific incidents that led her to feel this way towards her landlady, Ahilya?"

"Nothing in particular, but she did mention that when Sakshi was leaving Ahilya's apartment, Ahilya took her photo. It struck us as odd. Sakshi asked her why she was photographing her, and Ahilya explained that she was keeping a record of the girls who stayed in her apartment, making it easier for other girls to rent the space."

"That does sound peculiar."

"We thought so too, but in Mumbai, we figured such things might happen. As Sakshi was new to the city, she agreed to it."

"Alright." Samrat diligently recorded the pertinent information.

"Oh yes, she also spoke about a friend who was her roommate when she first rented the room."

"What was her name?"

"Kanak. She mentioned that her roommate Kanak was peculiar and different from the other girls."

At the mention of Kanak's name, Samrat's attention sharpened, momentarily puzzled. But then he quickly reasoned that there were likely numerous women named Kanak.

"And what about Kanak?" he inquired with intrigue.

"Sakshi mentioned that her behavior set her apart from the others. She was quiet, enjoyed her own company, and was always engrossed in her books."

The traits described by Sakshi's mother inexplicably reminded Samrat of his own wife, Kanak.

"Do you happen to have any pictures or something of Sakshi's friend that you mentioned?" Samrat, leaning in with anticipation, inquired.

"I don't recall much, but when Sakshi first entered her room, she sent me some photos of the place. I can show you if it might help." Sakshi's mother replied.

"Yes, please."

Sakshi's mother went inside to retrieve her phone.

"Here you go." She handed the phone to Samrat, already opened to the photo section.

"Sorting through these photos might take a little time," she warned.

"Yes, I suppose so," Samrat agreed with a smile.

All the photos were stored in Google Photos, which made the process more convenient for Samrat. He filtered out the unrelated ones, focusing only on those spanning an eight to ten-year period. He carefully examined each photo, hoping to spot Sakshi's friend. Whenever he came across a photo with Sakshi and a female friend, he turned to Sakshi's mother, inquiring about the person's identity. However, each time, it turned out to be someone other than the girl Sakshi had mentioned.

"Are you certain she sent you photos of her living quarters?" Samrat asked, his patience wearing thin.

"I did mention it might be among these, but I can't be sure," she replied.

"Alright," Samrat continued to scroll.

After five minutes of scrolling, an image appeared on the screen depicting a wall covered with photos. He kept scrolling and found more pictures of the same place. In one, Sakshi had captured a table with four drawers, and in the next, she'd photographed two entrances to different rooms.

As Samrat examined the photos of the table and the entrances, he had a sudden realization. He took out his phone and opened the photo he had taken in the burnt apartment. He compared each image and confirmed that they were indeed from the same apartment he had visited.

Intriguingly, he kept scrolling and stumbled upon a photo of a bed piled with clothes, with a girl seated behind it. Her face was clearly visible, and Samrat was taken aback when he saw it. He gasped in astonishment.

He turned the phone towards Sakshi's mother.

"Is this the girl? Sakshi's roommate?"

"Yes, Sakshi took this photo when I asked her if she needed more money for clothes. She sent me this, saying she had enough for the time being."

"The girl?" Samrat focused on the image.

"Yes, that's her, Sakshi's former roommate."

"Would you mind if I saved this photo on my phone?" Samrat asked. She nodded in agreement.

Sitting in his car, Samrat gazed at the photo, particularly studying the girl captured in the candid moment. It was a picture of Kanak, seated on the bed with a pile of clothes kept in front of her.

A recent day found Kanak in solitude within her apartment, realizing that further distractions were futile. It seemed prudent to defer the remainder of the resolution to Samrat's judgment. Nonetheless, she contemplated confiding a few crucial details to her mother, who had played a significant role in Kanak's concealed history.

"Mom, I'm afraid Samrat has begun to harbor suspicions about me," Kanak confessed anxiously over the phone.

"What do you mean? Didn't you plan things out?" Her mother's voice seethed with anger.

"I did, and I thought it might work in my favor, but it didn't. What should I do now?" Kanak's voice trembled, tears welling in her eyes.

"If you had informed me of your situation earlier, I would have never involved you with a police officer. But you always keep things to yourself, always!" Her mother's tone was laced with frustration.

"Now, when things are spiraling, you choose to confide in me. Honestly, Kanak, what's come over you?" Her mother's voice held a mix of exasperation and concern.

"Enough, Mom. I didn't call to be scolded, alright? If you can help me, then help. Otherwise, let me deal with this on my own. It was your excessive worrying that made Samrat doubt me in the first place," Kanak burst out.

"Kanak! Stop this attitude. It will lead you nowhere, do you understand?"

"I'm sorry, but can you please refrain from pointing out my mistakes and just help me, Mom?"

"I don't see a solution, Kanak. I don't think you have any options left to escape."

"What do you mean?"

"I mean you either run away or confess to Samrat."

"It wasn't a crime. It was self-defense, Mother. At least you understand that."

"I'm sorry. I think you should leave this situation and go somewhere where you're not known to anyone."

"I can't do that. I can't leave Samrat."

"He won't drop the case, and if he discovers your involvement, he won't back down."

"Regardless, I can't abandon him like this. And even if I confess, it will be up to him whether to arrest me or understand my reasons. But I can't keep him in the dark any longer."

"Don't let your emotions cloud your judgment!"

"You know I always make decisions with my head, and this time is no different. I'm going with what my instincts are telling me," Kanak replied calmly.

"You don't understand, you haven't done anything wrong, and it was years ago. You shouldn't have to suffer for it."

"If Samrat believes me, he won't let me suffer. If he thinks I'm guilty, then it's his call to make. I'll accept it. I'm tired of hiding, of carrying this secret, of enduring my nightmares alone. Remember when I came to you after finishing my education? I pleaded with you not to tell anyone about my Master's degree. It was because I was trying to distance myself from that dreadful day. I used to lie awake at night, crying. You never came to check on me because I never wanted to appear weak in front of you and Baba.

Then I married Samrat, and things began to change. I started finding joy in life with him, even though he wasn't always there. But when he was, it felt like the whole world was bright. I love him to my life."

"Initially, I harbored a sense of apprehension upon learning that Samrat was relocating to a locale I had previously inhabited, despite the considerable distance from her residence. The world, as they say, is small, Mom. For days, I maintained a reticent demeanor, fearful of the potential revelation to Samrat. However, as time elapsed, the situation gradually eased, and he remained unaware. It's a testament to the inevitability of facing one's actions within the same lifetime. Just when stability seemed restored, he encountered Ahilya. I am aware of my innocence in this matter, yet it weighs heavily that my husband is a police officer"

"I'm not with you in this, Kanak. I don't agree with your decision."

"I want you to promise me that no matter what happens to me, you and Baba will never blame Samrat for anything."

"Kanak..."

"No, Mom. I knew the day would come when I'd have to face this, and now it's here."

Kanak ended the call, tears streaming down her cheeks. All she could think of now was giving her confession to her husband.

CHAPTER 26
THE CONFESSION

The day Samrat returned from his journey was marked by a sense of staggering disbelief. His mind was flooded with a torrent of questions, each vying for attention, making it impossible to settle on one to ask Kanak.

"Kanak knew about Ahilya for so long, yet she never saw fit to mention it to me? Never? Sakshi, her dear friend, is gone, and she conceals the truth. Why?" Samrat pondered, feeling a mounting ache in his heart, his grip on the steering wheel weakening. Navigating through his apartment seemed a distant task; he was overwhelmed by a profound sense of despair and helplessness.

Just a few steps from his destination, he knew he was about to face his wife. There were so many questions he wanted to pose, so many truths he wished to understand - the lies she wove, the history she concealed. Yet, he also knew he couldn't compel her to speak. He couldn't bear the thought of witnessing her pain, seeing her tears. The questions would inevitably bring forth tears, and he couldn't bear to see her cry. And so, he made a conscious choice to let it all go - the inquiries, the past, the truth, and even Ahilya's case.

"If Kanak chose to keep this hidden, it must be something she never wanted me to uncover. I won't pry. I don't want to know," he whispered to himself, before pressing the doorbell.

Kanak greeted him at the door, her smile conspicuously absent.

"You must be exhausted. I'll prepare some tea for you," she offered, heading toward the kitchen.

Samrat trailed behind her.

"What's wrong?" she inquired.

"Nothing," he replied with a strained smile.

"Samrat, there's something I need to share with you. Something you should be aware of. It pertains to your case, Ahilya's case."

His gaze met hers, awaiting an explanation.

"I never shared anything about my college years with you, and you never inquired about my past. There's a dark chapter from my history, one I've tried to keep hidden from you. I thought I could go on living, concealing it, and find happiness, but it's recently resurfaced, haunting me once more," she confessed, a trace of remorse in her laughter.

"I never disclosed that I also pursued a Master's degree. I have it, but I asked my parents not to reveal it to anyone because it's tied to a past I wanted to leave behind. And I did, for many years. But I think now is the time. I'm about to share something with you, Samrat. It's going to hurt, shatter you. After hearing it, I leave the decision to you. Whatever you choose, I'll accept it."

"While at K.M University, studying biomedical engineering, I rented an apartment near the college. It was owned by Ahilya. When I arrived, she was strict and somewhat rude. To convince me that many other girls had rented from her, she showed me agreements and their photos. I thought it might be the norm in this city. The next day, another tenant arrived, Sakshi. We were told to share a room, but she wasn't my friend, never was. Still, we shared that space. She was outgoing, a free spirit, wanting to savor every moment, while I was the complete opposite, always engrossed in a book.

As months passed, Sakshi grew weary of Ahilya's rudeness and constant complaints. She found it unbearable to stay in the same apartment with Ahilya, so she moved in with her boyfriend. Before leaving, Ahilya asked if she could take a photo for record-keeping, a request I found peculiar. Yet, I didn't dwell on it and carried on, as Ahilya had offered to pay only half the rent. It was a relief, as it meant I could focus on my studies without worrying about accommodation. Little did I know, it was all part of her scheme.

One evening, returning from my part-time job at a shop, I discovered a stranger lounging on Ahilya's couch. When I asked who he was, he responded rudely and began to impose himself on me. He claimed to love me, finding me attractive and appealing. I'd never seen him around the apartment or the building. He then revealed that Ahilya, whom I'd come to regard as a decent companion, was involved in human trafficking. She'd take pictures of girls she deemed marketable. I refused to believe him, as I had no idea who he was and his words sounded preposterous. But then, he showed me those pictures, and as I examined them, he overpowered me, he... he assaulted me, and he continued until..." Kanak's voice caught, her throat tightening.

"I took a knife and attacked him, slicing his throat. I killed him," she confessed, her eyes brimming with tears. Yet, she was determined not to let them show to Samrat. She wiped her eyes and continued.

"After a while, Ahilya entered the apartment and found me with the man's lifeless body. His blood stained me, the knife still in my hand. She was in shock, seeing him lying there, dead. She was a different person - not the Ahilya I had confided in. This was a desperate, love-struck woman, revealing her true nature before me. When she learned that I had killed him, she flew into a rage and advanced toward me, consumed by madness, intent on ending my life. All I could do was defend myself, and in the struggle, I pushed her into the table. Her head struck the corner, and she collapsed to the ground. I believed she was dead, but upon checking, I found she was only unconscious. So, I brought her to my room, bound her to a chair with rope, stuffed her mouth with cloth, and sealed it with tape to prevent her from making any noise. Later that night, I moved the man's body to Ahilya's bathroom, where there was a bathtub. The next morning, I couldn't deviate from my routine. I attended college, worked, and returned home. At work, I asked my employer to lend me a chainsaw. He was puzzled, but I concocted a story about a DIY project, crafting a desk for my studies, and he bought it. That night, I resolved to dismember the body and hide the parts in a place they'd never be found. I knew the noise of the chainsaw might awaken Ahilya, so I gave her a sizable dose of sleeping pills, hoping they'd take effect. It took me three days to reduce his body into manageable pieces, easily disposed of."

Samrat finally broke his silence, asking the question that hung heavily in the air, "What did you do with those parts?"

"There's a garden not far from that building. After work, I went there, buried the pieces, and sowed seeds in the soil after each burial. People commended my efforts, never suspecting a thing," she recounted.

"And Ahilya? What about her?"

"I hadn't known she'd lost her memory, as I always kept her sedated. Once I was done with disposing of the man, I finally allowed Ahilya to regain consciousness. It was then I realized she had no recollection of events. I interpreted it as a sign from a higher power, an assist from fate. I decided to conclude everything on a favorable note. I rented a new place and took Ahilya with me. Next, I sold items that hadn't been consumed by the fire - a bathtub, some showcases, metal plates, and the like. Following that, I set the entire place ablaze as planned. Afterward, I deemed it unsafe to keep Ahilya with me, so I staged an injury and had her admitted to the hospital. Prior to that, I'd confirmed that she'd never be able to recall what had transpired that night."

"Kanak--" Samrat's voice trailed off, his eyes wide in disbelief. It was difficult for him to fathom that a woman could execute such a plan.

"I'm sorry, Samrat. I kept this from you," Kanak murmured, dropping to her knees.

"I evaded confronting this haunting reality until you brought me back to this city. The prospect of returning to a once-shunned locale filled me with trepidation and left me speechless. I couldn't confess to you, I was afraid. I'm sorry. I believed that serenity would prevail, and we could forge a good life together until her unexpected return disrupted our peace." She continued.

Tears flowed freely, her hands shielding her face from Samrat's gaze. Her heart was weighed down, an ache coursing through her body.

Unable to bear her distress, Samrat rushed to his wife's side, joining her in tears. "You did nothing wrong, Kanak. They deserved this."

Kanak looked at Samrat in astonishment.

"Yes, they deserved it, and I'm proud of you. You did nothing wrong. All I see is that you saved countless other girls from her."

"Samrat--" Kanak clung tightly to her husband, tears streaming down her face.

"Shh--- I won't let you happen anything and no one will ever touch you again. I told you even if the world is against you I will stand by your side. Don't you ever worry about this thing, okay?" he assured, cradling her in his arms.

In his embrace, Kanak found solace and security. She believed every word he spoke, trusting that he would shield her. She believed that her husband would protect her and would always be there even if the world went against her.

Now, it was Samrat's responsibility to handle everything. He resolved to shield his wife from anyone who might be privy to this case. The first order of business was to convince Madhav that the girl he was seeking was deceased. To safeguard Kanak, he decided to employ the name Sakshi instead. After all, mentioning a dead person wouldn't invite further scrutiny.

In a café, he sat waiting for Madhav, prepared to share the fabricated account. Samrat took a sip of his coffee, glancing outside. Madhav emerged from a cab.

"Hey," Samrat greeted, ensuring his voice carried enough for Madhav to hear and approach.

"Why did you call me so urgently?" Madhav inquired as he took his seat.

"This is quite urgent and crucial for you to understand the person responsible for what happened to your mother," Samrat began. Madhav leaned forward, elbows on the table, fingers intertwined, listening intently.

"The girl who inflicted harm on your mother was the final tenant who resided with her. Her name was Sakshi. She had come to realize your mother's involvement in such activities and feared she might be the next target. This could have led to a confrontation between Sakshi, Ahilya, and her partner."

"Partner?"

"Yes, Lalit. The mention of his name drove your mother to lose control. Sakshi was responsible for Lalit's demise in the accident. Subsequently, she kept your mother captive. It's possible that during this time, your mother fell, injuring her head, which ultimately resulted in her memory loss."

"Where is she now? How did you find out about this?"

"I conducted some investigation, Madhav. Remember, I am a police officer." Samrat smiled.

"Sakshi is no longer in this world. Her parents informed me she met with a fatal accident." He continued.

Madhav smirked, masking his inner turmoil.

"I suppose your search is now complete. Even if you could have apprehended the perpetrator, your mother would have ended up in prison for her actions against those girls."

"Yes, in any case, thank you, officer. You've assisted me when no one else cared to, and I appreciate you for telling me the truth."

'The truth' Samrat thought and extended a hand to shake Madhav's.

In the evening, upon Samrat's return to their apartment, he discovered Kanak was not there. He called out for her but received no response. An unsettling feeling washed over him, anxiety creeping in at not finding his wife at home. He quickly dialed her number and heard the phone ringing from the bedroom - she had left it behind.

"I hope she's alright. Where could she have gone?" he muttered, growing increasingly anxious.

The apartment door creaked open, and Samrat's ears caught the sound of approaching footsteps. He hurried to see who it was. To his immense relief, it was Kanak, accompanied by her mother. A wave of relief washed over Samrat as he approached his wife, enfolding her in a tight embrace, his concern outweighing any reservations he might have had about his mother-in-law's presence.

"I was so worried about you."

"Maa arrived this evening, so I took her out for a walk. I didn't expect you back so soon."

"That's alright. Hello, maa," Samrat warmly greeted his mother-in-law, bowing to touch her feet for a blessing.

"Thank you, Samrat, for everything you've done for her. I can never thank you enough for your kindness," Kanak's mother expressed, hugging her son-in-law.

"I won't let anything harm her. I promise," Samrat reassured with a smile.

That night, the three of them shared dinner together. Later, Samrat and Kanak escorted Kanak's mother to see her off. Upon returning home, Samrat found himself grappling with a question he wanted to ask Kanak. He hesitated, not wanting to dredge up painful memories related to Ahilya's case for his wife. Yet, when Kanak saw her husband's uncertain expression, she sensed there was something weighing on him.

"What's on your mind?" she inquired, standing before Samrat.

"Nothing," he replied with a smile.

"Please, tell me," she implored, cupping his face in her hands.

"Does Maa know about this? About Ahilya and--"

"Yes, but not everything. I only told her about Ahilya's part, not the murder."

"Good. Please, promise me you won't ever share this with anyone."

"I won't, I promise," she affirmed, smiling, and embraced him.

Samrat held her close, finding solace in their embrace.

"And what about Madhav, Ahilya's son?" Kanak inquired, walking alongside Samrat.

"Oh, I told him that Sakshi was the one who killed that man, and it was Sakshi who harmed his mother. Since Sakshi is no longer alive, he won't pursue further. Also, he discovered that his mother was involved in illicit activities, so he decided to put an end to it."

"Okay."

"And your department?"

"Oh, that won't be a problem. Besides, no one has any knowledge of it. I can come up with a plausible explanation."

"Thank you, Samrat. Thank you for everything."

Samrat gently took her hand and pressed a tender kiss to her fingers as they strolled toward their apartment.